Ghosts!

The Ultimate Guide for Ghost Hunters

Richard Brassey

Orion
Children's Books

First published in Great Britain in 2006
by Orion Children's Books
a division of the Orion Publishing Group Ltd
Orion House
5 Upper St Martin's Lane
London WC2H 9EA

A catalogue record for this book is available from the British Library.

Printed in Italy

ISBN 10 – 1 84255 527 8
ISBN 13 – 9 78184255 527 9

WHAT ARE GHOSTS?

All over the world – as far back as history goes and right up till now – people have believed in ghosts. Stories about ghosts have even been found in ancient Egyptian writing. This book tells you some of the weirdest ghost stories ever recorded.

What exactly *are* ghosts? Most people think ghosts are the spirits of dead people who have unfinished business. They get stuck between the living and the dead in a place called *limbo* where they are terrifically unhappy. Now and then, they pop back to this world. Often they want to tell anybody who can see them about their problem.

People who can see ghosts are called *psychics*. But just as not everybody can see ghosts, not all ghosts can see people.

One idea is that ghosts who can't see people are just like recordings. Something so terrible happened to them when they were alive that their feelings burst out of their bodies and were recorded in the surroundings. Hundreds of years later a psychic person, visiting the same spot, may be mysteriously able to see a complete action replay of the terrible event.

In books and films, ghosts sometimes try to hurt people. But although ghosts can be extremely scary, there's no evidence that they can actually hurt anyone.

People who don't believe in ghosts say they're easy to explain. They nearly always appear at night but nobody can see clearly in the dark. Feeling a chill doesn't prove there's a ghost because everybody feels a chill when they're scared. Ghost photographs can be faked.

All the stories in this book are taken from accounts by people who say they saw ghosts. You can make up your own mind whether to believe them or not.

GHOSTS FALL INTO TWO GENERAL CATEGORIES

INTERACTIVE GHOSTS

Can we talk?

. . . are eager to communicate with the living

NON-INTERACTIVE GHOSTS

I think you are very rude!

. . . don't seem to notice living people

To find out about the different forms ghosts take, turn the page.

TYPES OF GHOSTS

And where to find stories about them in this book …

GHOSTLY PEOPLE

You may not realise that they're ghosts until they do something impossible, like walk through a wall. Sometimes, they're see-through – a dead giveaway!

APPARITIONS

Any ghost that you can see.

PHANTOM HITCHHIKERS

They ask for a lift but mysteriously vanish during the journey.

GHOSTS WITH UNFINISHED BUSINESS

Something bad happened in life, which they need to fix.

TIMESLIP GHOSTS

They always do the same thing, just like a recording of something that happened long ago.

ANNIVERSARY GHOSTS

Appear once a year on the exact date when something terrible happened.

FAMILY GHOSTS

Attach themselves to a particular family. Sometimes they foretell a death or misfortune.

He's just like one of the family.

GHOSTLY ANIMALS

Animals can become ghosts too.

GHOSTLY PLACES

Some places are like a magnet to ghosts, spirits and phantoms.

GHOSTLY OBJECTS

Not all ghosts were once alive …

It looks real to me!

GHOSTLY WORDS YOU'LL NEED TO KNOW

DARK ENTITIES
Mysterious shadows often only seen out of the corner of your eye.

DEMONS
Spirits of dead people who cause upset and unhappiness.

DOPPELGANGERS
Look identical to a living person and can cause trouble in places that person has never even been. Could be useful to blame things on!

ECTOPLASM
The see-through stuff ghosts are said to be made from. Nobody has ever been able to collect any to analyse in a laboratory.

ENTITIES
The essence of pure evil. Some say they were never even human.

EXORCISM
A ritual performed in a haunted place which is supposed to send ghosts packing.

GHOST WRITING
Sometimes ghosts try to make contact with written messages.

ORBS
Are thought to be souls of dead people – they are usually photographic.

PHOTOGRAPHIC GHOSTS
Ghosts that only show up in photos.

POLTERGEISTS
Demons who get inside people so bad things happen wherever they go – like furniture flying around.

SÉANCE
A meeting in which people sit around a table to communicate with the dead.

SPIRITS
Usually harmless. Feels like somebody is in the room with you.

COULD YOUR HOUSE BE HAUNTED?

Do you wake in
terror in the small hours?

Do you glimpse moving shadows
out of the corner of your eye?

Do you feel you are
being followed or watched?

Do you hear noises or voices but
can't explain where they come from?

Do doors suddenly
open or close for no reason?

Do the lights turn on or
off by themselves?

Do you find things in strange places and
can't explain how they got there?

Do you feel a sudden
chill in some rooms?

Do you sense somebody invisible
in the room with you?

Does your cat behave oddly?

If you answered **YES**,
read on! The next page
gives you tips on how
to hunt for ghosts
at home.

Ghost-Hunting Equipment

Cotton thread and tape – so you can tell if doors have been opened in the night.

Windchimes – so you can listen out for approaching ghosts who cause a slight breeze.

Talcum powder – so you can see ghost footprints (*even though you might not see the ghost!*).

A mirror – so you can watch in more than one direction at once.

Your pet dog, because everyone knows dogs can see ghosts when people can't!

First-aid kit – in case of accidents in the dark.

A mobile phone – to call for back-up, although ghosts can block the signal – or to take photographs.

A thermometer – to record drops in temperature when you feel a sudden ghostly chill.

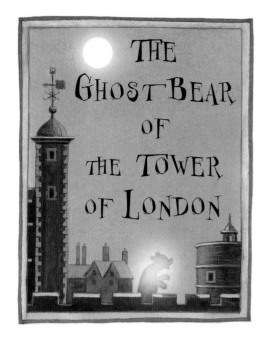

THE GHOST BEAR OF THE TOWER OF LONDON

One night in 1816 two sentries marched back and forth as usual outside the Tower of London where the Crown Jewels were kept.

They had just passed each other when one of them glimpsed, as the moon appeared briefly from behind a cloud, what looked like dark smoke seeping underneath the door.

Climbing the steps in pitch darkness for a closer look, he was astonished, as the moon peeped out again, to find himself face to face with a gigantic bear.

The bear reared on its hind legs and lunged. Frantically the sentry stabbed out. His bayonet passed straight through . . .

The bayonet stuck, quivering uselessly in the door behind, as the bear enveloped the sentry in a terrifying ghostly bear hug.

When the other sentry came marching back, he found his partner had passed out on the steps. The sentry recovered consciousness only long enough to tell what had happened. He died two days later.

Two hundred years ago there was a zoo in one of the twenty ancient towers which make up the Tower of London. Here many wild animals were cramped into small cages while unthinking people stared and teased them and made their short lives a misery. Perhaps the bear was the ghost of one of those unhappy animals.

In the British Museum there's a coffin lid on which is painted a woman's face.

Nobody knows what happened to the coffin. It's thought to have contained the mummy of a priestess of the scary Egyptian god, Amen-Ra.

It's all nonsense.

Utter rot!

Balderdash!

There are many peculiar stories about this lid which officials at the British Museum are eager to deny.

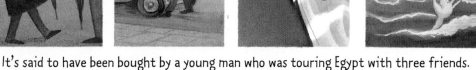

It's said to have been bought by a young man who was touring Egypt with three friends. All four met gruesome deaths very shortly afterwards.

The man's belongings, including the lid, were returned to his sister in England. No sooner had it entered the house than frightful things began to happen.

I sense terrible evil.

When Madame Blavatsky, the famous clairvoyant, paid a call, she sensed such evil that she advised getting rid of it. The British Museum agreed to take it.

The removal man who took the board to the museum died a week later.

The man who helped him carry it in had a near fatal accident.

A photographer took some photos but, instead of the painted face on the lid, they showed a real face, so evil-looking that he promptly committed suicide.

Not long after, another photographer suffered a series of unfortunate accidents with his equipment.

Meanwhile the museum attendants heard whistling, and refused to stay in the same room with the lid at night.

It caused so much trouble, the story goes, that the museum had it replaced with a replica. They sold the real lid which was shipped to the USA aboard the ocean liner, Titanic! There are those who say this is why the Titanic hit an iceberg and sank.

The British Museum once had its own Underground station where passengers often reported seeing the ghost of an ancient Egyptian late at night. Could it have been the priestess of Amen-Ra?

It's even said a secret tunnel links the station to the museum. We shall never know for the station itself is now a ghost. It was abandoned and sealed up over sixty years ago.

The lid floated to the surface and was taken aboard another ship which also promptly sank. That was the last time anybody saw the lid of the coffin of the priestess of Amen Ra . . .

It's all lies!

It never left!

The officials still insist that the lid has never left the museum.

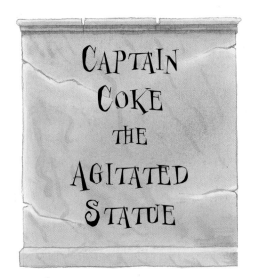

CAPTAIN COKE THE AGITATED STATUE

The marble statue of Captain John Coke stands on a fine, high pedestal in the church at Ottery St Mary in Devon. It is life-sized and made from many coloured marbles.

The captain was a man of wealth and importance.

Rumour has it that when he died, one night in March 1632, it was at the hand of his younger brother, who was after his money.

Though murder has never been proved, the captain certainly doesn't seem to be at peace.

Witnesses say that every year at midnight on that same night in March, his statue comes to life. He steps down . . .

. . . and runs agitatedly about the church . . .

. . . before returning, at length, to his pedestal.

THE ENDLESS TEARS OF LADY BLANCHE DE WARREN

In April 1264, a handsome knight named Ralph de Capo was engaged in some much-needed archery practice beneath the frowning walls of Rochester Castle.

Letting fly an arrow, he failed to notice his fiancée, Lady Blanche de Warren, enjoying the early spring sunshine in the gardens beyond. The arrow went wide. It whistled past the target and struck Lady Blanche who let out a small cry. Ralph raced to her side. Too late! She died right there in his arms.

That very night her ghost, dressed in a white gown and weeping endless tears, was seen upon the battlements. It is said she has been sighted every year since on the anniversary of that sad event.

THE PHANTOM LEGIONARIES OF YORK

As he worked in the cellar of an old house in York, plumber Harry Martindale was startled to hear the distant sound of a horn. He was rather more startled, a minute later, when a Roman soldier on a large horse came riding out of the solid stone wall. The horse was immediately followed by a platoon of Roman foot soldiers carrying spears.

At first Harry thought the legionaries were marching on their knees. But, in the middle of the cellar floor, there was a big hole where some archaeologists had recently dug down and uncovered a section of Roman road.

Harry realised that when the soldiers came to this, they were in fact marching at the level of the ancient road, as if the modern floor did not exist.

When they reached the far wall, they disappeared into that . . . as though it did not exist, either.

Harry dropped his tools and catapulted up the stairs, crashing straight into the caretaker of the house.

"You've seen them then!" said the caretaker, who seemed not the least surprised. He told Harry he was not the first person to see the soldiers . . .

In the 1920s the owners of the house threw a spectacular fancy-dress ball. The guests played games and wandered freely. One lady strayed into a narrow passageway in the cellar, where she came upon another guest, dressed as a Roman soldier. He seemed not to notice her. Despite repeated requests, he made no effort to let her past. She fled upstairs and complained to the hosts: "Who is that rude man dressed as a Roman soldier?"

"But none of our guests came as a Roman soldier, my dear!"

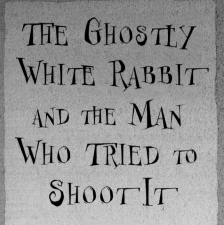

THE GHOSTLY WHITE RABBIT AND THE MAN WHO TRIED TO SHOOT IT

The ghost of a white rabbit haunts the churchyard at Egloshayle in Cornwall. As far back as memory goes, it has been seen dashing between gravestones at the time of full moon. Nobody seems to know the reason why.

Several attempts have been made to catch it – none more foolish than the efforts of a man who tried to shoot it. So eager was he that he tripped and shot himself instead.

Nowadays at full moon at Egloshayle you may see two ghosts: the small white rabbit and the man who tried to shoot it.

BARBARA CARTLAND AND THE VANISHING CASTLE

Barbara Cartland, who lived to be one hundred, wrote more than seven hundred books and was once the world's most popular author.

She often told the story of how, as a young woman, she'd taken a holiday with her brother in Austria. One sparkling summer's morning they had set out on a long ramble through the picturesque countryside. Coming upon a lake, late in the afternoon, they spied a fantastic castle on the opposite shore, its reflection shimmering in the glassy water.

"A storybook castle complete with spires and turrets," is how Miss Cartland described it.

It was too far to walk around the lake that day. But, back in the village where they were staying, they asked the innkeeper about it. He looked startled. It appeared there had once been a castle across the lake but it had fallen into ruin hundreds of years before.

After starting off next day at sunrise the Cartlands were amazed to find, on the spot where they had seen the castle, there was nothing but a pile of stones.

Barbara Cartland often saw ghosts. Her husband died many years before she did, but his ghost always appeared on their wedding anniversary with a large bunch of flowers. Also, she saw the ghost of her favourite spaniel, Jimmy — and so did all her other dogs who would chase around the garden with his ghost, just as they had when Jimmy was alive.

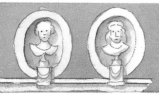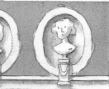

For four centuries Ham House has stood gaunt and lonely beside the Thames at Richmond. Should you ever visit you'll know at once it must be haunted.

On the dark oak-panelled walls are several paintings in which there's a King Charles spaniel with long floppy ears.

Don't be surprised if a dog just like it trips you on the landing or scampers by in the Hall Gallery.

It may even try to eat your sandwiches as it did to one lady who was picnicking on the terrace.

Visitors often complain – for dogs are not permitted in the house. But the caretaker cannot keep out ghost dogs!

People used to say this ghostly mutt was the pet of the wicked Duchess of Lauderdale who poisoned her first husband.

The ghost of her second husband also appears. He annoys visitors by smoking, which is not permitted either!

There are so many stories of ghosts at Ham that the Ghost Club of Great Britain once decided to spend a night there.

As the caretaker showed them round, everyone except Lance sniffed a strong smell of roses.

The Duchess's bed gave Tom and Rosie a creepy sensation.

In the Steward's Hall they noted the Fifth Earl's wheelchair. No one can explain how it moves from room to room in the night.

After a break to compare notes over coffee in the kitchen, things began to hot up.

Paulo whispered that a man in a yellow suit was following him out of the chapel.

On the stairs Greg came face to face with a girl in white who told him she'd been stabbed to death.

Finally, just before dawn, Joanne tripped over a floppy-eared spaniel in the Hall Gallery. She instantly recognised the dog in the paintings.

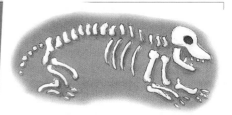

During recent work at Ham, a small skeleton was found buried under the floor of the Orangery. Bone experts say it may well be that of a King Charles spaniel. Today the bones can be seen in the Hall Gallery. It's now thought the ghost dog must be the one in the picture with Grace, Countess of Dysart, nearby.

THE LEAF-RAKING WOMAN OF CHAMONIX

Anybody who went travelling about Europe in the reign of Queen Victoria took a guidebook by John Ruskin with them.

Ruskin instructed people on the buildings and paintings and places they should find beautiful. His favourite place for writing his books was in the beautiful valley of Chamonix beneath Mont Blanc, the highest mountain in Europe.

Here, one day, he was told of a remote spot where the ghost of a woman was sometimes seen, raking leaves. She wore a shawl that hid her face and – this was the thing – she could only be seen by children.

The following day Ruskin sent his servant over to the next valley to borrow a child who had never heard of the ghost, so there could be no chance of pretending to have seen her.

Ruskin then set off with the child to where the ghost was said to appear. "How bracing and lonely a place," said Ruskin.

"There's not a living soul here but ourselves."

"There's that woman over there raking leaves." The boy pointed.

"Shall we approach her?" whispered Ruskin, trying not to sound too surprised since he saw no one. He took the boy firmly by the shoulders and pushed him in the direction he'd pointed. They had gone only a few steps when the boy suddenly froze.

No matter how hard Ruskin pushed, the boy refused to go a step further.

"What is it?" hissed Ruskin.

"She looked up," quavered the boy. "She's got holes instead of eyes. Her face is a skull!"

THE HAUNTED CHAIR OF OLD BATTERSEA HOUSE

"Who is that gentleman wearing fancy dress?" asked Lady Randolph Churchill, pointing to an oak chair across the hall while taking tea at Old Battersea House in London. Her hostess, Mrs Wilhelmina Stirling, saw nobody.

"Great heavens! Who was that just whispered in my ear?" exclaimed a guest on another occasion, leaping up from the very same oak chair as though electrocuted.

From then on Mrs Stirling, who lived to be a hundred, took to entertaining her guests in the Garden Room.

However, the small daughter of one such guest, happened to wander unnoticed into the hall and immediately came racing back. "Who's the man in a funny hat sitting in the chair?"

Mrs Stirling and her guest followed the child back into the hall. The chair was unoccupied.

"He's gone now," said the girl.

On another visit to the house Lady Churchill remarked, "Wilhelmina, you do seem to have a lot of guests who go to fancy-dress balls! I just passed somebody on the stairs who was dressed as my husband's long-dead ancestor, the Duke of Marlborough."

"I should hardly think anybody would be going to a ball at four in the afternoon," replied Mrs Stirling.

IGNATIUS, THE GHOSTLY BELL RINGER

Soon after the Bradshaws moved into Elm Vicarage at Wisbech in Cambridgeshire, they found themselves repeatedly woken at 3 a.m. by somebody ringing a bell. This set off Kik, who wouldn't stop barking.

Reverend Bradshaw investigated and found an unusual antique bell in the attic. But the ringing continued.

Do look where you are going!

Shortly after this, Mrs Bradshaw bumped into Ignatius for the first time. He seemed a bit irritable.

Another day she was sitting in the living room with her daughter Suzette. Ignatius strolled in and sat on a chair, whereupon Kik jumped into his lap. Suzette was astonished. Since she couldn't see Ignatius, Kik appeared to be suspended in thin air.

You're most welcome in our house.

Next time they met, Mrs Bradshaw determined to ask Ignatius all about himself. She wasn't scared, but he was rather embarrassed. Being a monk, he wasn't used to talking to a woman. But this is the story he told . . .

Seven hundred years before, there had been a monastery where Elm Vicarage stands today. The nearby river often overflowed its banks, so the monks would take turns to watch from a tower and ring a warning bell if the monastery was in danger. One night, when it was Ignatius's turn, he fell into a deep sleep.

He awoke to find the river had suddenly risen and was flooding. Frantically ringing his bell, he raced downstairs only to be swept away and drowned along with many of his brethren. Since then, his ghost had wandered in anguish.

Some weeks later when her husband was away, Mrs Bradshaw was woken in the night by Kik snarling. She opened her eyes to see a dark figure who tore off the bedclothes and began throttling her.

The next thing she realised, Ignatius was wrestling the dark figure. Then, just as suddenly, he and the figure vanished. In the morning Mrs Bradshaw had several purple bruises on her neck.

She met Ignatius in the passage some while afterwards but his image was rather faint. He told her the dark figure was the ghost of a murderer. He said that saving her had made him feel much better about failing to ring the bell, and that he wouldn't be quite so restless in future. Indeed, Mrs Bradshaw seldom saw Ignatius again.

31

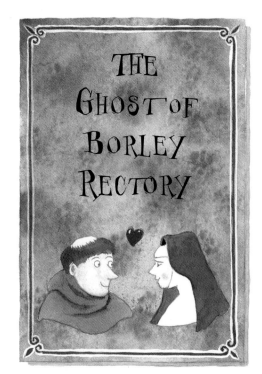

THE GHOST OF BORLEY RECTORY

Eight hundred years ago a monk fell in love with a nun. The two of them made plans to elope but were caught. The monk was hanged. Far worse, the nun was bricked up alive in the cellar of Borley Monastery.

Over time the monastery fell into ruin until in 1862, the rector, Henry Bull, announced he was going to build himself a new rectory on that very spot.

On the first night Reverend Bull's family sat down to dinner in their new dining room, the tormented face of the ghostly nun appeared at one of the windows. The Rev Bull had the window bricked up.

A series of ghostly events followed, which terrified Reverend Bull's daughters and servants. However, he and his son, Harry, found them entertaining. They would repair to the summerhouse after dinner and watch for the ghost as she flitted about the garden.

Harry became rector upon his father's death. He found it increasingly difficult to keep servants, especially after a coach and horses materialised without warning in the dining room.

In 1930, Reverend Lionel Foyster and his wife, Marianne, moved in, and all hell broke loose. Furniture changed places of its own accord. Objects flew through the air. Windows smashed. There were odd noises in the night. Marianne was slapped about the face by invisible hands.

She was thrown out of bed.

Messages addressed to her began appearing on the walls in hard-to-read handwriting.

The Foysters left.

It was at this point that the celebrated ghost-hunter, Harry Price, arrived with a team of forty volunteers. Day and night they watched. Every type of ghostly activity was recorded. During a séance, they received a message from a nun, named Marie. She said she was buried in the cellar.

In another séance, a spirit announced that the rectory would burn to the ground.

A year later, after Harry had left, the new tenant knocked over an oil lamp and the whole place went up in smoke. Onlookers saw the nun at one of the windows while the flames raged about her.

Today few traces remain of the most haunted house in England. But, before the nettles and weeds moved in, Harry Price returned and dug down into the cellar. Here he discovered the bones of a young woman. He arranged a Christian burial for them and the ghostly nun has not been seen since. Perhaps she is finally at peace.

THE HEADLESS WOMAN OF ST JAMES'S PARK

On the darkest nights there rises from the lake in St James's Park, near Buckingham Palace, the body of a woman in a red dress. She hovers above the surface until, reaching the shore, she races off, seemingly in a panic to find something she has lost.

This should perhaps not be too surprising for she has no head.

The story goes that two hundred years ago a sergeant in the Guard murdered his wife by decapitation. No one knows where he buried the head but he threw her body into the lake.

The bewildered ghost terrifies all who cross her path. On one occasion it took several weeks in hospital for two stout Coldstream Guards to recover from such a meeting.

In 1810, at St James's Palace, the Duke of Cumberland claimed he woke one night to find his servant, Mr Sellis, attacking him with a knife. The Duke said he fought him off. Soon after, Sellis was found with his head almost sliced from his body. Did he commit suicide or did the Duke have him murdered? Nobody knows — but Sellis still haunts the palace corridors, his wound spurting, leaving behind the stench of blood.

In 1972 a taxi driver, swerving to avoid her as she dashed in her frenzy across Birdcage Walk, hit a lamppost and was arrested for dangerous driving. When the magistrate heard how many witnesses have seen this headless woman over the years, he accepted the driver's story without question and the charges were dropped.

PETER, THE REMOVAL VAN GHOST

Stop messing about, Colin!

They believed him to be the ghost of Peter, an elderly Greek man who had lived in the flat before them. After Peter died, his body lay undiscovered for several months.

Peter seems to have grown strangely fond of Roberta. When she had to spend a few weeks in hospital, Peter drove Colin up the wall with his banging until she came home.

But it was when they decided to move house to Bolton that Peter really went berserk. "He started thumping the bed," says Roberta.

Roberta and Colin Davies' London flat was haunted. At first, Roberta had thought the ghost was Colin playing tricks on her. "He wasn't frightening so much as annoying," says Roberta. "He'd hang around and stand right behind me."

But then she saw the ghost in the hall. He wore a long, dark overcoat and a wide-brimmed hat which hid his face.

36

Finally, the removal men arrived to collect their furniture and they set off on the long drive up the motorway to Bolton.

Imagine Roberta's amazement when, only a few days after they'd settled in, she caught a glimpse of a familiar dark figure in the hall of the new house. She's certain that Peter must have sneaked into the removal van.

Roberta has grown so used to Peter that these days she says she'd probably miss him if he wasn't there.

37

HOW TO KEEP GHOSTS AWAY

When life gets a little too spooky . . .

Wearing lucky stones – such as jade and obsidian – can ward off evil spirits.

The burnt leaves of the Indian neem tree keep ghosts at bay. So do the leaves of the banyan tree.

Carrying salt in your pocket is a popular preventative.

It's well-known that ghosts hate looking in mirrors.

An iron horseshoe (or an iron rod placed in a grave) will stop ghosts in their tracks.

A light spray of mist from a water bottle will keep ghosts away for twenty-four hours, as will a sprinkle of talcum powder.

In some cultures people distract ghosts by wearing red underwear or shoes.

Sergeant Young was never surprised when motorists came into Annan police station to report running people over in the middle of the night. He grew up near the A75 and knew very well that it's the most haunted road in Scotland.

Donna Maxwell was sure she'd hit a man in a red jumper who appeared in front of her car. But Sergeant Young could find no trace. Several other people have reported seeing the same man in the middle of the road.

Mr and Mrs Miller told Sergeant Young they'd run down a man, wearing a sack on his head, but there was no sign of him either.

Mr and Mrs Ching were driving to Gretna to be married when an old Victorian woman appeared in front of them in a cloud of mist. Their car went right through her.

A Dornock woman saw an old man leaning against a wall beside the road. When he turned to face her, he had black holes where his eyes should have been.

A lorry driver was sure he was too late when he screeched to a halt to avoid squashing a couple who were kissing in the road – but there was no sign of them when he leaped from his cab to look.

Derek and Norman Ferguson were driving home one midnight when a hen came flapping towards their windscreen, then suddenly vanished.

It was followed by an old lady, a screaming, long-haired man, cats, dogs, a goat, more chickens and several creatures they never knew existed. All of them vanished just as they were about to hit the windscreen.

The car started rocking and the air turned a bitter chill.

When Derek got out to investigate, a furniture van came bearing down on him out of nowhere. He thought he was a goner . . . but it too disappeared. Not surprisingly, many of the locals take the long way round to avoid travelling the A75 late at night.

MRS PIGGOT'S GHOST CHASES A BICYCLE

Mr and Mrs Piggot lived near Newport in Shropshire. They had only one child, upon whom both doted.

One evening, Mrs Piggot, a tall woman, was about to enter the living room, when she overheard Mr Piggot say to a visitor, "If ever I had to choose between the death of my wife or my child, I hope it is my wife would die."

Mrs Piggot was so taken aback she ran shrieking from the house. She sprinted down the nearby tree-lined avenue, known as Windy Oaks, and without further ado drowned herself in a pond.

After that terrible night, whenever the wind blew through the leaves of the oak trees, people would say they could hear her shrieks. Some even claimed to have seen her ghost.

Late one evening a young man was cycling home along Windy Oaks when he had the uneasy sensation of being followed. Glancing over his shoulder, he caught sight of a tall woman running behind him.

Something about her terrified him, but the faster he pedalled to get away, the more she seemed to gain until she had drawn level and was running right alongside. Then, with a sudden shriek, she veered from the road and vanished towards the pond. Silence descended broken only by the rustling of leaves. The young man didn't hang about . . .

Practise your story first by reading it aloud.

Try to learn some lines off by heart so you can watch your audience closely.

Find some props to make spooky noises.

Choose an eerie beginning, like, 'It was a dark and stormy night …'

Darken the room, and shine a torch towards your face as you speak.

Whisper to make the audience listen closely – especially towards the end.

Ask a friend in the room to scream when the tale is told!

ENGLAND'S HAUNTED PALACES

British royals are used to seeing their ancestors amongst the ghosts in their palaces …

HAMPTON COURT PALACE

At least thirty ghosts haunt the maze of rooms that make up Henry VIII's huge palace. Three of Henry's wives appear – Anne Boleyn, Jane Seymour (carrying a candle) and Catherine Howard. Among the others is a lady in old-fashioned dress who joins groups of tourists. They usually imagine she's an actor until she walks right through one of them.

THE HAUNTED GALLERY

After Henry VIII decided to get rid of his fifth wife, Catherine Howard, he shut her in her rooms. But one morning she escaped and raced to the chapel where she knew he would be. In a frenzy she banged on the locked door and begged him not to have her head chopped off until the guards dragged her shrieking back to her room. Henry never once looked up from his prayers.

Catherine's ghost has appeared so often in the passage outside the Chapel where this scene occurred that it is known as the Haunted Gallery. Tourists often report feeling chills and a sense of unease at this spot. Several have even been known to faint in terror.

SKELETOR, THE CCTV GHOST OF HAMPTON COURT

In 2003 two security men raced to investigate an alarm at Hampton Court Palace which meant some fire doors had been opened. But the doors were securely shut. So they played the recording from a TV camera which had been pointing at them.

As they watched, the doors burst open. Then a spooky figure appeared from inside and pulled them shut. From watching footage from other cameras, the guards are certain nobody could have been in that part of the palace at the time. They nicknamed the figure Skeletor.

WINDSOR CASTLE

Among the twenty-five ghosts at Windsor Castle, Elizabeth I and Charles I frequent the library. Charles's head is on his shoulders – odd, because it was chopped off. George III gazes from a window of the room where he was kept when he went mad, and Henry VIII walks through a wall.

THE TOWER OF LONDON

In its thousand-year existence the Tower has been fortress, palace, prison and place of death and torture. No wonder some say it has more ghosts than any other building in the world.

THE TWO PRINCES

In 1483, twelve-year-old Edward V and his brother disappeared from the part of the Tower known as the Bloody Tower because of all the gory stuff that went on there.

For centuries nobody knew what had happened to them until two small skeletons were found in a chest under some stairs. Many believe their uncle Richard III had them smothered in their sleep so he could steal the throne of England. Their ghosts often appear in their former prison – but if you try to comfort them they fade away, sobbing into the wall.

THE CHOPPED-UP COUNTESS OF SALISBURY

When the Countess of Salisbury refused to kneel at the block, the executioner chased her round it and hacked her to pieces. Her ghost is still seen suffering this awful fate on that very spot.

HEADLESS ANNE BOLEYN

Henry VIII's second wife, who was beheaded at the Tower, is the most often seen ghost ever!

When the executioner held Anne's head up for the crowd, her lips and eyes were still moving. They quickly shoved her body into a chest and buried it in nearby St Peter's Chapel.

Her headless ghost – wearing an empty bonnet – often materialises out of the gloom to the terror of the sentries.

One night a sentry, investigating a light in St Peter's, fell off a ladder after he saw Anne's ghost leading a procession of phantom Tudor ladies and gentlemen down the aisle.

Anne's ghost is seen in many places. Every year she arrives at her birthplace, Blickling Hall in Norfolk, in a phantom coach drawn by headless horses with a headless coachman.

Introduction

Welcome

Welcome to *Ready 2 Rumble: Prima's Official Strategy Guide*. Want to hop right in and release some tension? Head for a quick fight in Arcade mode. Feel like starting your own gym and guiding your stable of boxers to the top? Championship mode will fit the bill. No matter what the aim of your game is, *Ready 2 Rumble* is the boxing game you've been waiting for—over the top, in your face, and tons of action.

SET HIM UP FOR THE SHOT ...

... THEN LAND THE PUNCH AND SEND YOUR OPPONENT REELING.

STAND BACK AND TALK A LITTLE TRASH, BUT MAKE SURE YOU'RE ON THE OTHER SIDE OF THE SCREEN. OTHERWISE, YOU LEAVE YOURSELF WIDE OPEN FOR ATTACK.

IN CHAMPIONSHIP MODE, YOU MUST TRAIN YOUR BOXER TO REACH THE TOP.

YOUR OPPONENT HAS LANDED A CRUSHING BLOW. SHAKE IT OFF AND GET BACK IN THERE. YOUR FIGHTER STARTS OUT WITH NO RANK. AFTER WINNING THE BRONZE CLASS, YOU MOVE TO THE SILVER, THEN THE GOLD.

READY 2 RUMBLE FEATURES 17 BOXERS YOU MUST MASTER TO WIN.

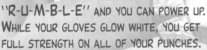

LAND A PUNCH WITH FULL POWER AND RECEIVE A LETTER. SPELL OUT "R-U-M-B-L-E" AND YOU CAN POWER UP. WHILE YOUR GLOVES GLOW WHITE, YOU GET FULL STRENGTH ON ALL OF YOUR PUNCHES.

TAP ANY BUTTONS TO GET YOUR ENERGY BACK AND GET BACK UP WHEN YOU SEE SOMETHING LIKE THIS.

How to Use the Guide

This guide starts off with "Gameplay Basics" to get you ready for your first fight. "Roll Call of Fighters" gives you the stats, moves, and all the strategies for each of the boxers. Check out "The Champ" for detailed information on your ultimate test. "In The Gym" is your guide to starting up your own gym and getting it to world class status. Next, find a chapter containing information on the PSX and N64 platforms. Finally, there's a chapter with special codes.

NOW LET'S TURN THINGS OVER TO RING ANNOUNCER MICHAEL BUFFER.

Gameplay Basics

The Basics

Before you step into the ring for the first time, you must learn a couple of the basics. Without them, you just might wind up getting your block knocked off. Familiarize yourself with the controller, a couple of the basic punches, blocking, RUMBLE mode, taunting, and fight pacing. These are all skills you must master before facing the Champ.

ANGEL "RAGING" RIVERA™ DELIVERS A BLOW TO BUTCHER BROWN™. THE PUNCH IS GOOD ENOUGH TO EARN RIVERA A LETTER FOR RUMBLE MODE. GET ALL SIX LETTERS AND YOUR PUNCHES LAND WITH MAXIMUM STRENGTH.

"FURIOUS" FAZ MOTAR™ HAS HIT AFRO THUNDER™ WITH A BLOW THAT SENDS HIM REELING.

AFRO THUNDER BLOCKS HIGH (R) HERE AGAINST TANK THRASHER™. BASED ON TANK'S STANCE, THUNDER HAS PICKED THE WRONG BLOCK. TANK'S NEXT BLOW WILL BE A BODY BLOW.

DUCK! THE PUNCH DOESN'T CAUSE YOU ANY DAMAGE IF YOU DUCK OUT OF THE WAY.

WHEN YOUR FIGHTER IS IN RUMBLE MODE, YOUR GLOVES GLOW WHITE, AND YOUR PUNCHES HIT WITH MAXIMUM STRENGTH.

YOU CAN TAUNT YOUR OPPONENT BY PRESSING EITHER ⓧ+Ⓐ OR Ⓨ+Ⓑ.

Punches

Your fighter has four basic punches at his disposal: High Left Punch, High Right Punch, Low Left Punch, and Low Right Punch. Combine them with either the D-pad or the control stick to increase the number of punches you can throw. From both left and right hands, you can throw uppercut, hook, and overhand shots to the body. Once you get these punches mastered, you can move on to the special moves for each fighter. The special moves pack a wallop and help you reach your ultimate goal, the Championship mode. See "Roll Call of Fighters" for the button combinations of all of the special moves.

Caution

The bigger punches (hooks, uppercuts, and special moves) all take a lot of time to execute. However, the payoff is big since they do great amounts of damage. You are vulnerable to attack while executing them, and a quick jab can stop your move cold. Try and land some traditional punches and combos (left jabs followed by right ones) at the beginning of the fight. When your opponent gets weaker or the guard drops, give it all you've got.

A BASIC LEFT HAND JAB (X)

A BASIC RIGHT HAND JAB (Y)

ANGEL RIVERA SETS UP FOR A LEFT HAND BODY BLOW (A) AGAINST BUTCHER BROWN.

ROCKET SAMCHAY™ LANDS A RIGHT-HAND BODY BLOW (B) WHILE FIGHTING SALUA TUA™.

ROCKET SAMCHAY SWINGS AN UPPERCUT (→+X) AT AFRO THUNDER.

SAMCHAY JUST LANDED A BIG RIGHT HOOK (↓+Y) ON SULA.

ROCKET SAMCHAY LANDS A FORCEFUL BODY BLOW (↓+A) ON SALUA.

TANK THRASHER LANDS A TENDERIZER (←,←,→+B) ON AFRO THUNDER.

TIP

Against the computer, keep your block up and let the opponent come to you. Absorb the first punch with the block and counter with a quick jab.

Blocking

Let's face it, throwing punches is one thing. Winning a fight is another. To win you must avoid your opponent's punches. Standing toe-to-toe with your adversary is suicide unless you are clearly the superior fighter. To become that superior fighter, you'll have to learn to duck and block. You can either block high (R) or low (L). Keep in mind that an opponent in RUMBLE mode, or one who is throwing a haymaker type punch (hook, uppercut, or special move), can penetrate your meager block. To avoid this situation, combine the blocks with a direction on the analog stick/D-pad. A high block (R) and any direction causes your fighter to duck his head. A low block (L) and any direction causes your fighter to jump out of the way.

A CASE OF DOUBLE VISION? NO, JUST BUTCHER BROWN FIGHTING BUTCHER BROWN. THE BUTCHER ON THE RIGHT IS ATTEMPTING A HEAD BLOCK [R] AGAINST THE OVERHAND RIGHT OF THE BUTCHER ON THE LEFT.

THIS CAMERA ANGLE MIGHT BE FUN TO TRY, BUT IT'S NOT VERY GOOD FOR THE LONG HAUL. YOU CAN'T SEE ENOUGH OF THE RING TO BLOCK EFFECTIVELY.

AFRO THUNDER SHOULD HAVE PULLED BACK (←+[R]) TO AVOID THE ONCOMING JAB OF "FURIOUS" FAZ MOTAR.

PROBABLY THE EASIEST WAY TO BLOCK IS TO NOT BE THERE. MOVE AWAY FROM A FIGHTER AS A SPECIAL MOVE STARTS, AND THE BLOW HITS NOTHING BUT AIR.

AFRO THUNDER LANDED A LEFT HOOK (↑+ⓧ) THAT WENT RIGHT THROUGH BUTCHER BROWN'S HIGH BLOCK ([R]).

RUMBLE Mode

If you can land a solid punch on your opponent, your fighter receives a letter. Get six letters and you spell out "R-U-M-B-L-E." When RUMBLE is complete, press [R]+[L] to put your fighter into RUMBLE mode. For a few seconds, your gloves glow white and you have unlimited power for a short time. Other things to look out for while in RUMBLE mode are listed below.

• Any letters you might be saving will go away at the end of the round, so use them before time is up.
• Be careful once you have knocked down your opponent. Usually, you'll press [R] and [L] to start rejuvenating your fighter. Just remember that if you have "R-U-M-B-L-E" spelled out, doing so will engage RUMBLE mode. Then once the other fighter is back up, your RUMBLE mode is wasted.
• Once you've got RUMBLE mode activated, make it count. Throw as many punches as you can. I recommend starting with an uppercut (←+ⓧ), which can be a great knockout blow.
• If your opponent has entered RUMBLE mode, back off. Dance about the ring and wait for the RUMBLE mode to wear off.
• Ⓐ + Ⓑ activates Rumble Flurry.

AFRO THUNDER'S UPPERCUT INFLICTS THE RIGHT AMOUNT OF DAMAGE. THAT EARNS HIM A LETTER "R"—ONLY FIVE MORE LETTERS TO GO.

BOTH BOXERS HAVE SPELLED OUT "R-U-M-B-L-E." TO ACTIVATE RUMBLE MODE, PRESS [R]+[L].

YOUR GLOVES GLOW WHITE AFTER ACTIVATING RUMBLE MODE. KEEP PUNCHING BECAUSE YOU HAVE UNLIMITED POWER.

BIG HOOKS LIKE THIS ONE HAVE A DEVASTATING EFFECT IN RUMBLE MODE.

WHEN YOUR OPPONENT IS IN RUMBLE MODE, BACK OFF. YOU DON'T WANT TO GET HIT WITH A FLURRY OF FULL-FORCE PUNCHES.

Taunting

Whether you are fighting a friend or the computer, taunting the opponent can bring a smile to your face. Each character has two taunts. The first is activated by Ⓧ+Ⓐ, and the second is accessed by Ⓨ+Ⓑ.

Caution

If you call for a taunt, make sure you are far away from the other fighter. Calling for a taunt with the other boxer in close invites a free shot. While taunting you can't block or move, allowing your opponent a chance to land a clean blow.

LULU VALENTINE™ TAUNTS BY DOING A CARTWHEEL ACROSS THE RING.

SALUA TAUNTS MOTAR HERE. SALUA IS DOING THE SMART THING BY HANGING BACK TO DO THE TAUNT.

JET "IRON" CHIN™ CALLS FOR A TAUNT, BUT "BIG" WILLY JOHNSON™ IS WAY TOO CLOSE.

JOHNSON TAKES THE OPEN SHOT AND SENDS CHIN FLYING BACKWARD.

Fight Pacing

An important skill to learn is fight pacing. *Ready 2 Rumble* is not just a game to mash buttons; you have to think a little. Pace yourself for maximum effect, and the Championship belt will be yours.

• When your opponent is in RUMBLE mode, back off, wait for it to expire, then head back in. Why feel the fury of his full-power punches?

• You gain more Health between rounds. So if you are getting close to running out of Health, run. Yes, I said *run*. Stay away from the corners and you can avoid being knocked down.

• Throw as many punches as you want. Your punch strength goes down with each punch thrown in rapid succession.

With Angel Rivera in RUMBLE mode, Butcher Brown needs to hang back until Rivera's gloves stop glowing.

Boris "The Bear" Knokimov™ is in big trouble here. The best strategy is to back off and wait for the end of the round. Your Health bar recuperates between rounds.

When you have an opponent staggering backward, keep pressing the advantage. Show no mercy.

Keep throwing those punches until you spell "R-U-M-B-L-E." This powerful uppercut will get you a letter.

Once in RUMBLE mode, keep the punches coming. Each one that scores a hit does maximum damage to your opponent.

Don't get caught in the corner like Butcher Brown here. You'll get pummeled.

VMU

The VMU is used to save games and show you data during the fight. You get Health, Punches Thrown, Hit Percentage, and Punch Strength in the palm of your hands during the fight. One of the ways to use the VMU is to watch your Health meter build back when your opponent is down. You must press the buttons as fast as possible for maximum effect. You can watch the VMU for the status of the Health bar, rather than watching the screen as you tap the buttons to increase your Health bar.

HEALTH BAR	
NUMBER OF PUNCHES THROWN	31
% OF HITS	12%
POWER BAR	

Here is the info you get from the VMU during a fight.

Roll Call Of Fighters
The Fighters

When you start *Ready 2 Rumble* you're given 14 fighters. Get each of your boxers to the Silver Class in Championship mode and you unlock the 15th fighter, Bruce Blade, the Bronze Class Champ. Take each of the boxers to the Gold Class in Championship mode, and the 16th fighter becomes available, Nat Daddy™, the Silver Class Champ. Get all 16 boxers to the Championship level and you will unlock the final fighter, Damien Black™, Champ of the Gold Class. Each boxer has his or her own strengths and weaknesses, but with the help of this chapter you will learn how to win as each of them. You will also get the pros, cons, and all of the special moves. If you can't defeat a particular boxer, check them out in this guide. There are tips on beating each of them, too! Damien Black, the final boxer you have to fight, gets his own section in "The Champ."

THE ROAD TO THE TOP IS A BUMPY RIDE. HERE MOTAR LANDS A QUICK RIGHT JAB ON BRUCE BLADE™. IF YOU ARE BRUCE, BACK OFF AND TRY TO WAIT IT OUT, OR GET KNOCKED DOWN.

LULU VALENTINE LANDS A QUICK UPPERCUT IN RUMBLE MODE, AND BORIS IS SENT FLYING BACKWARD. WHEN YOU ARE IN RUMBLE MODE, LAND AS MANY PUNCHES AS YOU CAN.

THE ARTWORK IN *READY 2 RUMBLE* IS INCREDIBLE. AFTER A FIGHT YOUR BOXER SHOWS THE DAMAGE. SALUA IS SPORTING A NICE BLACK EYE AFTER THIS CONTEST.

DAMIEN BLACK HOLDS THE CHAMPIONSHIP BELT FOR THE GOLD CLASS, AND YOU MUST TAKE IT AWAY FROM HIM.

AFRO THUNDER LANDS AN UP TEMPO MOVE IN THIS FIGHT AGAINST ROCKET SAMCHAY. LAND A SPECIAL MOVE IN RUMBLE MODE FOR A TRULY LETHAL BLOW.

SALUA IS IN BIG TROUBLE RIGHT HERE. IF YOU ARE SALUA, GET OUT OF THE CORNER. IF YOU ARE ROCKET SAMCHAY, KEEP HIM PINNED. ROCKET'S GOT HIM RIGHT WHERE HE WANTS HIM.

Notes

In order for the moves to work as they are listed, the character needs to be facing right. If you are facing left, just reverse the arrows.

Selene Strike

Notes

Selene is, pound for pound, one of the best female boxers in the world today. Her graceful technique is backed by lethal power, particularly with her potent straight and right hook. Not particularly fast, this young veteran makes up for her lack of speed with awesome toe-to-toe tactics.

The Stats

Hometown:	Brasilia, Brazil
Weight:	130 lbs.
Height:	6'2"
Reach:	80"
Age:	24

Fighting Basics

JIMMY BLOOD™ IS DOING BETTER THAN SELENE IN THIS FIGHT, SO HE DECIDES TO TAUNT HER.

BAD CHOICE. A QUICK JAB SHUTS HIM UP AND LEADS TO A FLURRY OF LANDED PUNCHES IF HE KEEPS IT UP.

SELENE STRIKE IS AN EXCELLENT BOXER. USE HER QUICK HANDS TO LAND LOTS OF JABS AND UPPERCUTS. THAT COMBINATION CAN BE DEADLY.

 MS. STRIKE DOES A LITTLE SPIN WHEN SHE STARTS RUMBLE MODE. NO MATTER HOW YOU GET THERE, THE EFFECT IS THE SAME.

 A DEVASTATING BLOW IS ON THE WAY.

 THE ONLY REAL PROBLEM WITH SELENE IS HER SLIGHT FRAME. SHE CAN'T ABSORB TOO MUCH OF A BEATING. USE HER BLOCKS AND DODGES TO KEEP VICTORY WITHIN YOUR GRASP.

Special Moves

Rush →,→

 TO EXECUTE A RUSH, MOVE A SHORT DISTANCE AWAY FROM YOUR OPPONENT.

 THEN PRESS THE COMBO →,→ TO CHARGE.

 COMBINE THE RUSH WITH AN UPPERCUT TO DO A TON OF DAMAGE.

No Love ←,→+Ⓑ

 SELENE STRIKE IS ABOUT TO GIVE BIG WILLY JOHNSON A SHOT ...

 ... THAT ISN'T EXACTLY FAIR.

 THE BLOW DOUBLES OVER JOHNSON. HEY THIS IS A FIGHT, WHO SAID IT HAD TO BE FAIR?

Rejection →,←+Ⓨ

 THE RIGHT HAND COMES BACK ...

 ... THEN FORWARD ...

 ... TO LAND TO THE HEAD OF JIMMY BLOOD.

Superwoman ←,→+Ⓧ

SELENE READIES FOR SUPERWOMAN BY MOVING IN CLOSE AND LOW ...

... AND BRINGS THE LEFT HAND UP TO BUTCHER BROWN'S JAW.

THE MOVE FINISHES WITH A FLOURISH. THIS MOVE IS EASY TO EXECUTE AND DOES A LOT OF DAMAGE.

Below The Belt →+Ⓑ

SELENE MOVES IN CLOSE TO DELIVER BELOW THE BELT.

THE MOVE IS EXACTLY WHAT IT'S NAMED, A SHOT BELOW THE WAISTLINE.

NOT EXACTLY FAIR, BUT IT GAINS YOU A LETTER. BESIDES, ISN'T ALL FAIR IN LOVE AND WAR?

Cold Shoulder ←,←,→+Ⓐ

SELENE STRIKE IS ABOUT TO GIVE "BIG" WILLY JOHNSON THE COLD SHOULDER ...

... WHICH IS A QUICK BLOW TO THE BODY ...

... THAT DOUBLES YOUR OPPONENT OVER.

Rumble Flurry Ⓐ+Ⓑ

WHILE IN RUMBLE MODE, YOU CAN PRESS Ⓐ+Ⓑ TO START A RUMBLE FLURRY.

LOTS OF HIGH DAMAGE PUNCHES ARE HEADED YOUR OPPONENT'S WAY.

Ready 2 Rumble™ Prima's Official Strategy Guide

How To Beat Her

SELENE'S PUNCHES ARE QUICK BUT DON'T DO A LOT OF DAMAGE. YOU CAN CHOOSE TO FIGHT THIS BOXER TOE-TO-TOE.

GO FOR BODY BLOWS. IT HELPS COUNTER-ACT HER QUICK DEFENSIVE JAB.

JUST LIKE WITH ANY OTHER BOXER, ENTER RUMBLE MODE WHEN YOU CAN. SELENE'S IN TROUBLE HERE.

AVOID MOVES THAT TAKE LARGE AMOUNTS OF TIME TO EXECUTE. A QUICK JAB CAN STOP YOUR MOVE DEAD IN ITS TRACKS.

WATCH OUT FOR SELENE'S QUICK RIGHT JABS. THEY MAY NOT DO MUCH DAMAGE, BUT THEY HURT NONETHELESS.

NOW THAT YOU'VE GOT THE STRATEGIES DOWN, HEAD BACK TO THE GAME AND GET READY 2 RUMBLE.

Boris "The Bear" Knokimov

Notes

Boris is a folk hero in his country along with being a living legend all across Eastern Europe. He is arguably one of the most complete fighters in the circuit with both inside and outside attacks. With the support of the best Olympic coaches and gyms in Croatia, Boris trains intensely for every fight, believing that he must never let his country down.

The Stats

Hometown:	Zagrev, Croatia
Weight:	220 lbs.
Height:	6' 3"
Reach:	73"
Age:	30

Fighting Basics

BORIS IS A POWERFUL FIGHTER. HIS HOOK DELIVERS A HECK OF A PUNCH.

RIVERA FEELS THE WRATH OF A RIGHT JAB. BORIS ISN'T THE QUICKEST OF BOXERS, BUT WHEN HE HITS, IT COUNTS.

THAT SAME RIGHT JAB PACKS ENOUGH OF A WALLOP TO STOP JIMMY BLOOD WHILE HE'S IN RUMBLE MODE.

BUTCHER BROWN GETS SENT FALLING BACK ...

... AND DOWN FOR THE COUNT.

THE UPPERCUT IS ANOTHER OF THE GOOD PUNCHES BORIS HAS IN HIS ARSENAL.

Special Moves

Superior ←+Ⓨ

SUPERIOR STARTS OUT WITH BORIS COCKING BACK HIS POWERFUL RIGHT HAND.

YOU CAN TELL THIS HOOK IS COMING BY THE WAY THE LEFT HAND TELEGRAPHS WHERE THE BLOW WILL BE GOING.

THE BLOW IS DELIVERED, AND RIVERA GETS SENT BACKWARD.

Justice Axle ←,→+Ⓧ

IT SEEMS LIKE ALL OF BORIS'S MOVES START OUT WITH A SPIN.

YOU ARE VULNERABLE DURING THIS, AND ALL OF BORIS'S MOVES. MAKE SURE THAT YOUR OPPONENT IS STUNNED OR FAR ENOUGH AWAY.

THE BLOW FINISHES WITH A LEFT TO THE BODY.

Reigning Axle →,←+Ⓨ

THE WAY BORIS STARTS HIS CURL, YOU'D THINK ANOTHER POWERFUL LEFT HOOK WAS COMING.

BUT IT'S THE RIGHT HAND THAT GETS RAKED ACROSS THE FACE OF "BIG" WILLY JOHNSON.

TAKE ADVANTAGE OF THE OTHER BOXER WHEN HE IS STUNNED LIKE THIS. MOVE IN AND THROW A QUICK JAB.

Salua Tua

The Stats

Hometown:	Waipahu, Oahu
Weight:	358 lbs.
Height:	6'0"
Reach:	77"
Age:	33

Notes

Salua is a former sumo wrestler who originally came from Hawaii but later moved to Japan to take on the world's greatest sumo wrestlers. After becoming grand champion, Salua was concerned with the lack of recognition sumo receives from the rest of the world. A consummate disciplinarian, he has entered boxing and left his championship behind in an attempt to represent and bring respect to the sport he loves.

Fighting Basics

Salua lines up for an overhand right to Rivera.

And he lands it. Salua is powerful yet slow. Use big punches like this one to get your letters for RUMBLE mode.

This is a quick uppercut. It doesn't take long to set up and is one of Salua's most effective punches. Here it catches "Raging" Rivera off guard, and Salua gets another letter.

SALUA JUST TURNS HIS BACK TO START RUMBLE MODE.

THIS LEFT HAND JAB LANDS AND SNAPS LULU'S HEAD BACK. ONCE YOU GET THE FIRST ONE TO LAND, PRESS THE ADVANTAGE AND THROW SOME MORE LEFT JABS. IT'S A SIMPLE PUNCH, BUT SALUA'S STRENGTH MAKES IT COUNT.

SALUA'S PUNCHES TEND TO BE TELEGRAPHED LIKE THIS ONE, SO YOUR OPPONENTS KNOW WHAT'S COMING. THEREFORE, MAKE SURE THEY CAN'T DO ANYTHING ABOUT IT. HOLD OFF THE BIG PUNCHES UNTIL OPPONENTS ARE STUNNED OR TRYING TO SET UP THEIR OWN BIG PUNCHES.

Special Moves

Porkchop ←,→+Ⓨ

SALUA DRAWS BACK HIS RIGHT HAND AT THE START OF THIS MOVE ...

... AND DELIVERS THE BIG RIGHT HAND BLOW. THE POWER THIS MOVE BUILDS IS CONSIDERABLE. BE CAREFUL WHEN YOU THROW A PUNCH LIKE THIS THOUGH. SALUA'S LACK OF SPEED LEAVES YOU VULNERABLE.

Ton of Fun ←+Ⓧ

SALUA DRAWS BACK FOR THE START OF THE TON OF FUN MOVE.

THEN HE DRAWS HIS HIPS BACK ...

... AND USES HIS WEIGHT TO HIS ADVANTAGE. THIS MAY BE THE LITERAL EXAMPLE OF A BODY BLOW, AS SALUA USES HIS CONSIDERABLE BODY TO DO ALL OF THE DAMAGE.

All You Can Eat →,←+Ⓧ

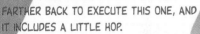

THIS MOVE IS AN EXTENSION OF TON OF FUN. SALUA DRAWS A LITTLE FARTHER BACK TO EXECUTE THIS ONE, AND IT INCLUDES A LITTLE HOP.

THIS MOVE DOES MORE DAMAGE THAN TON OF FUN.

Gut Buster →,←,→+Ⓑ

Salua winds up for a Gut Buster. The left hand sizes up the opponent.

And the right hand strikes Butcher Brown in the chest.

Monster ↓+Ⓐ,→,←+Ⓧ

Monster is a more powerful form of All You Can Eat. This variant starts out with a left to the body.

It's followed by the typical All You Can Eat belly smash.

The main difference is that this combo does more damage.

Rumble Flurry Ⓐ+Ⓑ

The Rumble Flurry is coming. Faz Motar retreats to get away from it.

But he can't get out of its way.

How to Beat Him

ATTACK THE BODY OF SALUA. A PUNCH TO THE GUT OPENS UP A PUNCH TO THE HEAD OR A SPECIAL MOVE.

SALUA'S MOVES ARE SLOW AND DELIBERATE. JET CHIN DUCKS UNDER THIS JAB ...

... AND FIRES BACK A QUICK BODY BLOW.

JIMMY BLOOD BACKS SALUA INTO THE CORNER. SALUA ISN'T VERY MANEUVERABLE, SO ONCE YOU GET HIM THERE, YOU SHOULD BE ABLE TO KEEP HIM PINNED.

YOU CAN DUCK OUT OF THE WAY OF MOST OF HIS PUNCHES. HERE, CHIN PULLS BACK ONCE HE SEES THE JAB IS COMING.

A QUICK BLOW TO THE BODY FROM LULU DOES THE TRICK. IT TAKES TIME TO KNOCK SALUA DOWN, BUT PUNCHES TO THE GUT ARE THE BEST WAY TO DO IT.

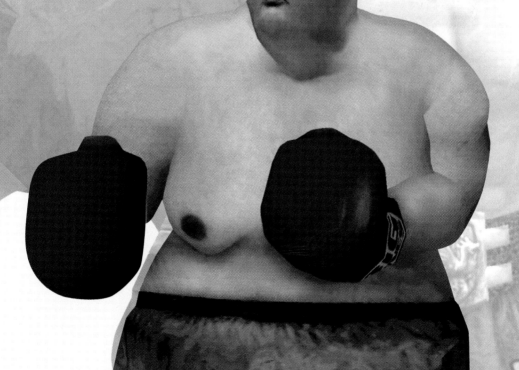

Tank Thrasher

Notes

Tank used to fight in the extreme sport of crocodile rodeo but soon got bored from the "lack of serious competition." Boxing is his forte now, and he has become a leading contender, often misleading opponents with his apparent lack of conditioning. Talking trash and pummeling opponents into submission, Tank holds up convincingly against the better-trained boxers.

The Stats

Hometown:	Guntersville, Alabama
Weight:	290 lbs.
Height:	6'4"
Reach:	80"
Age:	26

Fighting Basics

IF TANK ISN'T THE SLOWEST BOXER ON THE CIRCUIT, HE'S CLOSE. USE THE LEFT JAB TO START THINGS OFF RIGHT. TANK'S POWER ALLOWS HIM TO SLIGHTLY STUN HIS OPPONENTS WITH THIS JAB. HE CAN THEN FOLLOW WITH A NUMBER OF THESE IN A ROW.

TANK'S RIGHT JAB IS REALLY SLOW. HIS OPPONENT SAW THIS ONE COMING FROM A MILE AWAY.

THAT POWERFUL LEFT JAB WORKS TO TANK'S ADVANTAGE IN THIS FIGHT WITH SELENE. EACH ONE SNAPS HER HEAD BACK AND SENDS HER BACKPEDALING. NOW SHE'S TRAPPED IN THE CORNER AND WILL BE GOING DOWN SOON.

TANK VS. TANK? YOU HAVE TO FIGHT YOURSELF ON THE WAY TO THE CHAMPI-ONSHIP, WHICH MAKES FOR AN INTERESTING MATCH. STRENGTHS AND WEAKNESSES ARE THE SAME. CAN YOU OUTSMART THE AI?

THIS RIGHT HOOK GETS TELEGRAPHED, BUT BUTCHER BROWN CAN'T DO ANYTHING ABOUT IT. THIS PUNCH LANDS AND DOES A BUNCH OF DAMAGE.

THIS LEFT UPPERCUT IS A GREAT PUNCH TO USE WITH TANK.

Special Moves

Blitz ←+Ⓧ

BLITZ IS A GREAT MOVE. BOTH HANDS DRAW BACK ...

... AND START TO COME FORWARD ...

... AND BOX THE EARS OF YOUR OPPONENT. THIS MOVE IS EASY TO EXECUTE AND DOES A GOOD AMOUNT OF DAMAGE.

Rush →,→

YOU ARE FAR AWAY FROM SELENE IN THIS FIGHT. TO CLOSE THE DISTANCE QUICKLY, START A RUSH.

TANK DUCKS DOWN TO AVOID ANY PUNCHES THAT SELENE MIGHT THROW AND CLOSES THE DISTANCE. THIS MOVE DOESN'T DO ANY DAMAGE BY ITSELF; SEE THE NEXT FOUR MOVES FOR FINISHES TO THIS ONE.

Crash Test Right →,→+Ⓨ

THIS MOVE IS A FINISH TO THE RUSH.

THIS UPPERCUT CATCHES SELENE BY SURPRISE AND EARNS TANK A LETTER FOR RUMBLE MODE.

Roll Call of Fighters

21

Crash Test Left →,→+Ⓧ

THIS MOVE IS THE BASIC RUSH ...

... FINISHED WITH A LEFT UPPERCUT, WORTH ANOTHER LETTER HERE.

Shameless Left →,→+Ⓐ

THIS IS A RUSH, PLUS A LOW BLOW FROM THE LEFT. LIKE THE NAME OF THE MOVE, THIS IS A SHAMELESS ACT, BUT IT WORKS. SO WHY NOT USE IT?

Shameless Right →,→+Ⓑ

ANOTHER RUSH FINISH, THIS ONE IS A LOW BLOW FROM THE RIGHT SIDE.

Tenderizer ←,←,→+Ⓑ

THE TENDERIZER IS A SERIES OF BLOWS TO THE GUT ...

... RIGHT, LEFT, RIGHT, LEFT.

THIS SOFTENS UP ANY OPPONENT. NOW EAT HIM UP AND SPIT HIM OUT.

Rumble Flurry Ⓐ+Ⓑ

THE RUMBLE FLURRY SHOWCASES ALL OF THE SPECIAL MOVES.

SAVE IT FOR SPECIAL OCCASIONS.

How to Beat Him

... AND SPECIAL MOVES ...

... TO SEND TANK CRASHING TO THE CANVAS.

TANK CAN TAKE A LOT OF PUNCHES. SO TO BEAT HIM, THROW YOUR MOST POWERFUL PUNCHES ...

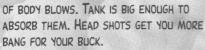

THIS UPPER-CUT FROM SELENE DOES THE TRICK. STAY AWAY FROM A LOT OF BODY BLOWS. TANK IS BIG ENOUGH TO ABSORB THEM. HEAD SHOTS GET YOU MORE BANG FOR YOUR BUCK.

WHEN YOU SEE TANK BACK OFF LIKE THIS, BE PREPARED TO DODGE OUT OF THE WAY. HE'S ABOUT TO DELIVER ONE OF HIS RUSH MOVES.

ALL THOSE BIG MOVES (UPPERCUTS, HOOKS, AND SPECIALS) GET YOUR BOXER TO RUMBLE MODE IN A HURRY. THE EXTRA POWER THAT RUMBLE BRINGS CAN HELP YOU KNOCK OUT TANK.

"Big" Willy Johnson

Notes

Willy comes to us from the late 1800's where he was the undisputed fist-a-cuffs champion. Brought to the present through a mysterious rift in time, he resurfaces among modern-day gladiators in an attempt to remind the world where the sport originated. From a time where there were hardly any rules, no time limit, and little protection, Sir Johnson serves up a rowdy blast from the past.

The Stats

Hometown:	Chester, England
Weight:	172 lbs.
Height:	5'9"
Reach:	72"
Age:	108

Fighting Basics

THEY JUST DON'T MAKE 'EM LIKE THEY USED TO! "BIG" WILLY MIGHT HAVE A SLENDER FRAME, BUT HIS PUNCHES PACK A WALLOP. THIS OVERHAND RIGHT TO BUTCHER BROWN ...

... SENDS HIM FLYING TO THE CANVAS.

WHILE JOHNSON IS FAIRLY QUICK ON SOME PUNCHES, HE'S NOT QUICK WITH MOVES LIKE THIS SETUP FOR AN OVERHAND RIGHT.

BORIS CAN SEE THIS MOVE COMING, BUT HE GOT CAUGHT TRYING TO SET UP HIS OWN PUNCH. LUCKY FOR JOHNSON HE GOT HIS PUNCH IN FIRST.

WILLY'S GOT A GREAT LEFT JAB. IT'S REALLY QUICK AND DOES A FAIR AMOUNT OF DAMAGE. SNEAK THE FIRST ONE IN AND KEEP THROWING A JAB. YOU CAN LAND A TON OF THEM.

JOHNSON'S LITTLE DANCE AFTER HE WINS A FIGHT SHOULD BRING A SMILE TO YOUR FACE. TO SEE IT, YOU MUST MASTER THIS WELL-ROUNDED BOXER.

Special Moves

Clockwork →,→,←+Ⓧ

INSTEAD OF A LEATHER BAG, YOU USE YOUR OPPONENT'S HEAD!

CLOCKWORK IS LIKE A ROUND AT THE SPEED BAG SESSION, WITH ONE LITTLE EXCEPTION.

AFTER A ROUND OF LEFTS AND A ROUND OF RIGHTS, THIS SPECIAL MOVE FINISHES WITH A LEFT HOOK.

Tea and Crumpets →,→+Ⓨ

...FOR A BIG RIGHT UPPERCUT.

THE MOVE FINISHES OFF WITH A BIG RIGHT HOOK.

... WHY NOT HAVE SOME FISH AND CHIPS? NO SERIOUSLY, THIS MOVE STARTS OUT WINDING UP ...

Stealing Props ↑,↓+Ⓧ or ↓,↑+Ⓧ

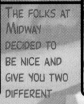

THE FOLKS AT MIDWAY DECIDED TO BE NICE AND GIVE YOU TWO DIFFERENT

THE FINISH IS A SWEEPING OVERHAND RIGHT.

WAYS TO COMPLETE THIS SPECIAL MOVE. IT STARTS OUT WITH A QUICK PUNCH TO THE CHEST.

Roll Call of Fighters

25

Old School ↑,↓+Ⓧ,Ⓐ or ↓,↑+Ⓧ,Ⓐ

THIS IS AN ADD-ON TO THE BASIC STEALING PROPS MOVE. AFTER THE LAST BLOW IS LANDED FROM STEALING PROPS, JOHNSON STARTS TO WIND UP WITH THE RIGHT.

THEN HE THROWS A LEFT JAB. THIS MOVE IS HARD TO EXECUTE; IT TAKES SOME TIME TO PRACTICE THIS ONE AND THE NEXT.

Timeout ↑,↓+Ⓧ,Ⓧ or ↓,↑+Ⓧ,Ⓧ

THIS IS ANOTHER FOLLOW-UP TO STEALING PROPS. IT FINISHES WITH A PUNCH TO THE GUT.

Rumble Flurry Ⓐ+Ⓑ

THROW THE RUMBLE FLURRY ONLY WHEN YOU ARE SURE TO HIT YOUR OPPONENT.

IT TAKES A LONG TIME TO EXECUTE, AND AN OPPONENT SIMPLY SLIDING OUT OF THE WAY CAN STOP YOU.

How to Beat Him

ONE OF THE BEST WAYS TO LEARN HOW TO DEFEAT A BOXER IS TO FIGHT A COUPLE OF ROUNDS AS THAT CHARACTER AND SEE WHAT THE AI OPPONENTS ARE DOING TO YOU. BODY SHOTS SEEM TO BE THE COMPUTER'S CHOICE, SO THEY SHOULD WORK FOR YOU AS WELL.

A QUICK SHOT TO THE HEAD WILL DO JOHNSON IN TOO. HIS SLIGHT FRAME MEANS HE CAN'T ABSORB A WHOLE LOT OF PUNISHMENT.

SALUA THROWS A QUICK UPPERCUT TO DISRUPT JOHNSON'S RHYTHM. JABS ARE REALLY QUICK PUNCHES FOR JOHNSON. HIS OTHERS ARE A LITTLE ON THE SLOW SIDE.

LULU HAS TO RESORT TO BIG PUNCHES TO TAKE DOWN THE BIGGER JOHNSON. USE YOUR BOXER'S STRENGTHS (IN THIS CASE, LULU'S BETTER SPEED) TO OVERCOME JOHNSON.

JOHNSON DOESN'T HAVE THE STAMINA TO GO TOE-TO-TOE WITH BIGGER FIGHTERS LIKE BORIS. TRADE BLOWS WITH JOHNSON IF YOU ARE THE BIGGER BOXER; YOU'LL COME OUT ON TOP.

BUT BE CAREFUL IF YOU DO; JOHNSON IS QUICK AND CAN COUNTER WITH A QUICK LEFT UPPERCUT.

Butcher Brown

Notes

Butcher is a goofy, cocky boxer who was once the undisputed champion, but lost his title in a controversial match with Boris Knokimov. After a leave of absence and a long bout with personal turmoil and disillusionment, an inspiring relationship with the spiritual Kemo Claw™ reunited him with the sport that once made him famous. Armed with newfound confidence, Brown is now determined to not only reclaim his belt, but to unify the championships as well.

The Stats

Hometown:	District of Columbia
Weight:	232 lbs.
Height:	5' 9"
Reach:	82"
Age:	23

Fighting Basics

BUTCHER BROWN IS THE PROTOTYPICAL BRUISER. HE'S BIG AND HE'S STRONG.

AND HIS LEFT JAB CAN BE LANDED WITH EASE AND REPETITION.

BUT THE REAL WORRY IS THE OVERHAND RIGHT HEADED LULU'S WAY.

EACH OF BROWN'S PUNCHES HAVE DEVASTATING POWER.

BUTCHER BROWN IS REALLY USING HIS HEAD. THIS IS THE END OF THE BAD MANNERS SPECIAL MOVE.

RUMBLE MODE JUST ADDS TO AN ALREADY IMPRESSIVE PUNCH. WHEN YOU GET RUMBLE MODE, DON'T HOLD BACK. LAND AS MANY PUNCHES AS YOU CAN.

SEE THAT FACE? BROWN CAN TAKE A LARGE AMOUNT OF PUNISHMENT, AS ILLUSTRATED IN THIS POST-FIGHT POSE. GO TOE-TO-TOE WITH THE OTHER BOXERS; BROWN CAN TAKE IT.

Special Moves

Brute Disaster ←+Ⓨ

BRUTE DISASTER IS A SIMPLE MOVE THAT DOES A GOOD AMOUNT OF DAMAGE. THE RIGHT HAND COCKS BACK ...

... AND COMES OVER THE TOP ...

... TO LAND A CRUSHING BLOW ON MS. VALENTINE.

Disaster Blaster ←+Ⓨ,Ⓧ

DISASTER BLASTER IS AN EXTENSION OF THE BRUTE DISASTER MOVE.

AFTER THE OVERHAND RIGHT BLOW IS LANDED, BUTCHER DROPS DOWN ...

... TO LET LOOSE THIS DEVASTATING LEFT UPPER-CUT.

Scrape The Gutter Ⓨ,Ⓧ,Ⓧ

HIS FIGHT STARTS OUT WITH A SCRAPE THE GUTTER MOVE. IT BEGINS WITH A RIGHT HAND JAB ...

.. FOLLOWED BY A LEFT HOOK ...

... AND COMPLETED WITH A LEFT UPPERCUT THAT SENDS LULU VALENTINE REELING.

Bad Manners ←+Ⓧ

BAD MANNERS IS A HEAD BUTT.

THIS IS A GOOD MOVE WHEN YOU ARE IN CLOSE QUARTERS WITH YOUR OPPONENT.

Total Disrespect ←+Ⓧ,Ⓐ,Ⓑ

TOTAL DISRESPECT IS A FOLLOW-UP TO BAD MANNERS. AFTER THE HEAD BUTT, BUTCHER BROWN THROWS A LEFT BELOW THE BELT ...

... FOLLOWED BY A RIGHT BELOW THE BELT. THAT'S NOT EXACTLY SPORTS-MANLIKE CONDUCT.

Wild Ride →,←+Ⓨ

READY TO GO FOR A WILD RIDE? THE FIRST STEP TO THIS COMBO IS A PIVOT BACKWARD.

AND THE BLOW COMES IN THE FORM OF A SWEEPING RIGHT HAND.

IT'S SURE TO TAKE THE STEAM OUT OF YOUR OPPONENT.

No Turning Back →,←+Ⓨ,Ⓧ,Ⓨ

NO TURNING BACK IS AN EXTENSION OF WILD RIDE BUT CAN ONLY BE COMPLETED IN RUMBLE MODE.

AFTER THE WILD RIDE PUNCHES ARE THROWN, BUTCHER LETS THE LEFT HAND DELIVER A SHOT TO THE HEAD ...

... FOLLOWED BY A BIG RIGHT HAND THAT SHOULD FLATTEN MOST OPPONENTS.

Rumble Flurry Ⓐ + Ⓑ

Butcher Brown feels the wrath of Butcher Brown.

Rumble Flurry is a way to see the special moves all wrapped into one.

How to Beat Him

Butcher's problem is that most of his big moves are too slow.

This gives quick opponents the option to either duck ...

...or counter with a quick punch of their own.

Butcher can take a pounding, so you have to unload big moves to do enough damage to knock him down.

Rocket delivers a RUMBLE mode enhanced left to do the trick against Butcher here.

Work the body of Butcher, it's his weakness. Just make sure you get in, throw the punch, and move back quickly. One of Butcher's blows at close range can ruin your day.

Jimmy Blood

Notes

A furious and malicious fighter, Jimmy is uncontrollable at the sound of the bell. While he's often criticized for his constant lack of discipline, no one can deny his fight-winning power and audacity among the professional ranks. His weapons of choice are devastating lunging hooks to the head.

The Stats
Hometown: Oamaru, New Zealand
Weight: 226 lbs.
Height: 6'2"
Reach: 87"
Age: 23

Fighting Basics

Jimmy cocks his hand back ...

This lunging left jab packs a good punch.

... for an overhand right. This move, like all of Jimmy's punches, takes advantage of his overall power.

Ready 2 Rumble™ Prima's Official Strategy

JIMMY'S NORMAL LEFT JAB IS NOT VERY QUICK. STICK TO MORE COMPLEX MOVES TO DISH OUT THE PUNISHMENT.

LIKE THIS RIGHT HOOK, FOR EXAMPLE. JIMMY IS VERY STRONG, AND THIS PUNCH WILL HURT.

THE BIGGER BLOWS ARE MORE DELIBERATE, SO HE'S WIDE OPEN FOR COUNTERATTACK.

Special Moves

Blood Rush ←,←,→+Ⓨ

START A BLOOD RUSH WHEN YOU ARE ABOUT THIS FAR AWAY FROM YOUR OPPONENT.

WHEN YOU'VE COMPLETED THE KEY SEQUENCE, JIMMY CHARGES TO CLOSE THE DISTANCE.

THEN HE LOWERS HIS SHOULDER TO KNOCK RIVERA BACKWARD.

Blood Shot →,←+Ⓑ

JIMMY CROUCHES LOW AT THE START OF A BLOOD SHOT.

THEN HE JUMPS UP HIGH.

FINALLY, HE STRIKES A CRUSHING BLOW TO BORIS KNOKIMOV.

Splatter Punch →,→+Ⓧ

THE SPLATTER PUNCH IS A LOT LIKE "BIG" WILLY JOHNSON'S CLOCKWORK.

THE PUNCHES COME IN RAPID SUCCESSION FOR MAXIMUM DAMAGE.

JIMMY BLOOD CAN REALLY DISH OUT THE PUNISHMENT; USE SPECIAL MOVES TO PUT YOUR OPPONENTS AWAY EARLY.

PROTECT THE BODY. RIVERA IS A GOOD FIGHTER BUT REALLY A LIGHTWEIGHT.

THE JAB KEEPS YOUR OPPONENT OFF BALANCE.

AND RUMBLE MODE PUTS HIM AWAY FOR GOOD.

DON'T GO TOE-TO-TOE WITH THE BIG BOYS, BUT YOU CAN PROBABLY TRADE BLOWS WITH A SMALLER BOXER LIKE AFRO THUNDER HERE.

Special Moves

Ghetto Blaster ←,→+Ⓧ

START THE SEQUENCE FOR THE GHETTO BLASTER RIGHT ABOUT HERE.

ONCE THE BUTTON COMBINATION IS COMPLETE, RUSH IN CLOSE AND GO INTO A CROUCH.

THEN EXPLODE UPWARD WITH A DEVASTATING LEFT UPPERCUT.

Lowrider →,←+Ⓑ

THE LOWRIDER STARTS OUT WITH A PIVOT BACKWARD.

WHEN RIVERA COMES AROUND, HE FIRES A QUICK RIGHT JAB TO THE BODY.

WITH THE MOVE COMPLETE, HE'S BACK IN A NORMAL FIGHTING STANCE. IF THE MOVE IS BLOCKED, YOU'RE IN BIG TROUBLE HERE, BECAUSE A COUNTER-PUNCH IS PROBABLY ON THE WAY.

Cruisin' →,←+Ⓑ,→+Ⓑ,Ⓐ,Ⓑ

CRUISIN' IS A FOUR-HIT LOW COMBO. IT STARTS WITH A SPIN PUNCH AND GOES INTO A RIGHT-HAND LOW ...

... THEN A LEFT LOW ...

... AND ENDS WITH A RIGHT HOOK TO THE BODY.

Salsa ➜+Ⓐ, ⬅, ➜+Ⓧ

SALSA IS HOT. START OFF WITH THIS POWERFUL LEFT BODY BLOW.

THEN THROW THE FAMILIAR GHETTO BLASTER ...

... FOR MAXIMUM EFFECT.

Lambada ➜, ⬅+Ⓑ, ➜+Ⓑ, Ⓐ, Ⓑ, ⬅, ➜+Ⓧ

LAMBADA IS A COMBINATION OF CRUISIN' AND GHETTO BLASTER.

FIRST THERE'S THE FAMILIAR SEQUENCE OF BODY BLOWS.

THEN RIVERA EXPLODES UP WITH THE GHETTO BLASTER TO FINISH OFF "BIG" WILLY JOHNSON.

Rumble Flurry Ⓐ+Ⓑ

ANGEL RIVERA LAUNCHES HIS RUMBLE FLURRY WITH TWO DIFFERENT RESULTS. IN THIS FIGHT, BORIS ATTEMPTS TO DUCK THE SEQUENCE.

ROCKET SAMCHAY ENGAGES HIS OWN RUMBLE MODE TO TRY AND COUNTERACT IT IN THIS FIGHT.

How to Beat Him

AFRO THUNDER WINDS UP A SUCKA PUNCH ...

... TO WORK THE BODY OF RIVERA. THAT'S THE WAY TO DEFEAT HIM. WORK THE BODY WITH SPECIAL MOVES ...

... AND COMBINATIONS TO KNOCK HIM DOWN. WATCH OUT FOR A COUNTER-PUNCH; RIVERA'S PRETTY QUICK.

JOHNSON USES HIS SPEED TO MOVE IN CLOSE, THROW A RIGHT TO THE BODY, AND MOVE BACK OUT AGAIN.

IF YOU HANG IN TOO CLOSE FOR TOO LONG, RIVERA SNAPS OFF A QUICK JAB TO THE HEAD AND SENDS YOU FLYING. BE CAREFUL.

USE YOUR SIZE TO YOUR ADVANTAGE. IF YOU'RE ONE OF THE BIGGER BOXERS, LIKE SALUA HERE, THROW YOUR WEIGHT AROUND AND DEAL OUT A HEAVY-HANDED BLOW.

Sucka Punch ↑,↓+Ⓨ,Ⓨ,Ⓨ,Ⓨ or ↓,↑+Ⓨ,Ⓨ,Ⓨ,Ⓨ

THE SUCKA PUNCH TAKES A *LONG* TIME TO EXECUTE. SO YOUR OPPONENT BETTER BE STUNNED OR NOT PAYING ATTENTION.

TAP Ⓨ AS THUNDER'S ARM COMES AROUND TO BUILD UP MORE POWER (AND HAVE THE MOVE TAKE EVEN LONGER). YOU CAN DO THIS UP TO THREE TIMES TO ADD MORE POWER.

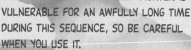

THE MOVE IS FINALLY OVER WITH THIS LANDED PUNCH. YOUR FIGHTER IS VULNERABLE FOR AN AWFULLY LONG TIME DURING THIS SEQUENCE, SO BE CAREFUL WHEN YOU USE IT.

Rumble Flurry Ⓐ+Ⓑ

THUNDER EXECUTES AN UP TEMPO MOVE WHILE IN RUMBLE FLURRY.

THE DAMAGE DONE IN RUMBLE MODE IS ALWAYS WORTH THE BUILDUP IT TAKES TO SPELL OUT "R-U-M-B-L-E."

How to Beat Him

AFRO THUNDER IS A LIGHTWEIGHT. DEAL OUT BIG, POWERFUL BLOWS LIKE SALUA DOES HERE ...

... AND BORIS DOES HERE.

BE CAREFUL THOUGH. AFRO THUNDER IS A VERY QUICK BOXER AND CAN SNEAK IN QUICK JABS TO UPSET YOUR RHYTHM. HERE THUNDER QUICKLY INITIATES UP TEMPO ON WILLY JOHNSON.

THUNDER IS EASY TO KNOCK DOWN.

JUST KEEP LANDING THE BIG MOVES, UPPERCUTS ...

... AND HOOKS. THUNDER CAN'T TAKE TOO MUCH PUNISHMENT.

Lulu Valentine

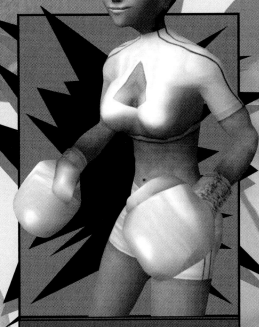

The Stats

Hometown:	Seattle, Washington
Weight:	105 lbs.
Height:	5'2"
Reach:	64"
Age:	21

Notes

A graduate student in business and fashion design, Lulu Valentine supplements her world famous clothing line with her other profession—prize fighting. Her compact and efficient punches generate surprising power that often catches opponents off guard. This, along with her stunning looks and knowledge, is more than enough to help her climb the ranks, where she hopes to make a name for herself and her business.

Fighting Basics

THEN COUNTER-PUNCH WITH A QUICK LEFT JAB.

LULU DOESN'T HAVE THE BODY TO ABSORB TOO MANY BLOWS. BLOCK THE PUNCH.

VALENTINE'S LEFT UPPERCUT IS QUICK. YOU CAN USE IT ALMOST LIKE A JAB. REALLY, IT'S THAT QUICK.

THE RIGHT UPPERCUT, THOUGH, IS REALLY SLOW. STICK WITH THE LEFT HAND FOR THIS KIND OF PUNCH. IT WORKS MUCH BETTER IN THE RING.

THE SAME IS TRUE FOR LULU'S BODY BLOWS. THE RIGHT HAND IS SLOWER THAN THE LEFT, DUE MOSTLY TO THE FACT THAT SHE TURNS HER BODY (BACK TO THE CAMERA HERE) TO THROW THE RIGHT-HAND BODY SHOTS.

THE LEFT-HAND JAB TO THE HEAD IS LULU'S BEST PUNCH.

LULU IS A GREAT BOXER. THE SIMPLE STRATEGY FOR WINNING WITH HER IS TO USE YOUR BLOCKS (R) AND (L) TO ABSORB THE PUNCH, THEN COUNTER-PUNCH WITH A QUICK JAB.

Special Moves

Springing Assault ←+ⓧ

LULU COILS UP TO UNLEASH THE SPRINGING ASSAULT.

THE LEFT HAND COMES OVER THE TOP ...

...TO LAND SQUARELY ON THE JAW OF BORIS KNOKIMOV.

Backhand →,←+ⓨ

MOTAR IS IN TROUBLE AS VALENTINE BRINGS HER LEFT HAND BACK AT THE START OF THIS MOVE.

VALENTINE'S HAND COMES FORWARD AND RAKES ACROSS THE FACE OF HER OPPONENT.

THIS IS A QUICK SPECIAL MOVE. YOU ARE VULNERABLE WHILE EXECUTING IT, BUT IT'S ONE OF THE SHORTEST TO CARRY OUT.

Triple Upper ←, ←, → + Ⓨ

You must be a little ways away from your opponent to execute the Triple Upper.

Once the combo is entered, Lulu springs forward, swinging her fists.

She lands the blow to the jaw of Jimmy Blood here.

Rumble Flurry Ⓐ + Ⓑ

Lulu's punches don't pack much of a wallop.

But combine RUMBLE mode with a Rumble Flurry to deal out unlimited punching power.

How to Beat Her

Selene lands a right jab here. Pick your spots to land punches against Lulu. She is a quick boxer and can score with a counter-punch when you least expect it.

Throw the big punches against Lulu. She can't absorb too much damage.

Get your moves in fast. Lulu's got a punch coming at the same time. Boris is too slow here, and Lulu's blow will land first, interrupting Boris's strike.

Fight your way through Lulu's blocks. Tank throws a left hand here that will get blocked, but keep it up.

Brown breaks through the block with this right hook.

And Selene breaks through with another right.

The Fighters

43

"Furious" Faz Motar

Notes

The former bodyguard of a wealthy Middle Eastern entrepreneur, Faz comes to the ring with a gritty, no-nonsense style. Fully backed by his wealthy benefactor, he is a cutting-edge specimen in the world of professional sports. Don't let the flashy garb fool you; he is dangerous both in and out of the ring.

The Stats

Hometown:	Riyadh, Saudi Arabia
Weight:	230 lbs.
Height:	6'5"
Reach:	76"
Age:	28

Fighting Basics

FAZ MOTAR'S STRENGTH IS IN HIS POWER. EACH PUNCH LANDED IS QUITE A HIT. HERE HE LANDS A RIGHT JAB.

FAZ CAN THROW A MEAN UPPERCUT TOO. THE LEFT-HAND UPPERCUT IS QUICKER THAN THE RIGHT.

THE JAB IS MOTAR'S MOST EFFECTIVE PUNCH. THROW A COUPLE LEFTS.

THEN THROW THE RIGHT FOR A GOOD ONE-TWO COMBO.

THIS OVER-HAND RIGHT RAINS TERROR FROM ABOVE. UNFORTU-NATELY, IT TAKES FOREVER TO EXECUTE, AND YOUR OPPONENT HAS TIME TO GET A BLOCK UP.

THIS LEFT HOOK IS A QUICK MOVE THAT CAN CATCH YOUR OPPONENT OFF GUARD.

Special Moves

Cruise Missile →, →+Ⓨ

CRUISE MISSILE IS A TWO-HANDED HOOK TO THE HEAD. TO EXECUTE IT, YOU NEED TO START FROM A DISTANCE.

MOTAR SPINS FORWARD ...

... AND STRIKES HIS OPPONENT WITH BOTH FISTS TO THE HEAD.

Urban Attack ↓, ↑+Ⓧ or ↑, ↓+Ⓧ

URBAN ATTACK STARTS WITH FAZ CURLING UP.

THEN HE UNLEASHES THE FIRST PART OF THIS MOVE, A BACKHAND LEFT TO THE HEAD ...

... FOLLOWED BY A RIGHT.

Whirlwind →, →, ←+Ⓧ

MOTAR CROUCHES IN FRONT OF JOHNSON HERE ...

... LANDING A POWERFUL LEFT UPPER-CUT.

Oasis →,→,←+ⓍＸ,→+Ⓨ

Oasis is an extension of Motar's Whirlwind move.

After landing the left uppercut, Motar ducks low.

Then he throws this right hand to the body of Jimmy Blood.

Rumble Flurry Ⓐ+Ⓑ

Each of the special moves is highlighted in Rumble Flurry.

Rumble mode gives you unlimited punching power.

Execute Rumble Flurry to send your opponent packing.

How to Beat Him

Beat Motar with blows to the body. Work him inside.

Then deliver a quick head shot like this uppercut.

Motar is a big boxer who can take a ton of punishment. Use your most powerful punches to wear him down.

Here Brown sends him back with a big right hook.

Use quick shots to disrupt his rhythm. Here Chin lands a quick jab to stop Motar in the middle of RUMBLE mode.

You can't take too many of Motar's punches. Use your blocks to survive longer.

Keep it up with big punches like this one. Motar can be beaten.

Jet "Iron" Chin

Notes

Jet once made a living as the stunt double for a famous Hong Kong movie star. After living in the shadow of his hero for many years, he made his way to the ring to make a name for himself outside of the theatre. Being new to the sport, Jet's lethal brand of martial arts often overrides his traditional boxing training.

The Stats

Hometown:	Taipei, Taiwan
Weight:	150 lbs.
Height:	5'8"
Reach:	78"
Age:	20

Fighting Basics

JET CHIN WORKS OVER BUTCHER BROWN IN THE CORNER. ONE OF CHIN'S BEST PUNCHES IS HIS RIGHT HAND TO THE BODY.

HE'S DOING IT RIGHT HERE TO JOHNSON TOO. WITH MOST BOXERS, YOU THROW REPEATED LEFT JABS TO SOFTEN UP YOUR OPPONENT. WITH CHIN, THROW REPEATED RIGHT JABS FOR THE SAME EFFECT.

CHIN'S OVERHAND RIGHT IS ALSO A GOOD PUNCH TO THROW. BACK YOUR OPPONENT INTO THE CORNER AND KEEP IT UP. IT'S A SLOW PUNCH, SO STUN YOUR ADVERSARY WITH BODY BLOWS AND COME BACK WITH THE RIGHT TO THE HEAD.

THE GREAT FANG IS ONE OF CHIN'S SPECIAL MOVES. HERE IT IS EXECUTED IN RUMBLE MODE FOR EXTRA POWER.

TO GAIN YOUR LETTERS FOR RUMBLE MODE, YOU MUST THROW THE BIG PUNCHES LIKE THIS RIGHT HOOK.

"IRON" CHIN CAN TAKE A PUNCH. GOOD THING TOO, BECAUSE THIS LEFT JAB FROM BORIS KNOKIMOV IS POWERFUL.

Special Moves

Firecracker ←+Ⓨ

CHIN'S HANDS COME OVER THE TOP ...

... TO STRIKE BROWN IN THE HEAD.

THE FIRECRACKER STARTS OUT WITH A SPIN. BE CAREFUL BECAUSE YOU ARE VULNERABLE WITH YOUR BACK TO YOUR OPPONENT.

Arch Protest ←+Ⓧ

CHIN CROUCHES AND BRINGS HIS LEFT HAND BACK.

HE THEN EXPLODES UP TO STRIKE AT JOHNSON IN THE HEAD.

CHIN'S PUNCH MISSED HERE. JOHNSON SAW THE PUNCH COMING AND MOVED BACK OUT OF THE WAY.

Giving Order →,←+Ⓨ

GIVING ORDER IS ANOTHER SPIN MOVE FOR CHIN.

HE JUMPS UP WITH THE RIGHT AND LEFT HAND COMING.

THIS BLOW STRIKES TANK ACROSS THE FACE WITH BOTH SHOTS.

Arch Nemesis ←+Ⓧ,Ⓐ,Ⓑ,Ⓨ

THEN HE RAKES HIS LEFT HAND ACROSS THE FACE OF AFRO THUNDER.

ARCH NEMESIS IS A QUICK SPECIAL MOVE. CHIN CROUCHES DOWN AND SPRINGS UP.

Great Fang ←,→+Ⓧ

CHIN REARS BACK ...

... AND GETS BORIS WITH A DOUBLE PUNCH TO THE BODY, A GREAT FANG.

Fists of Fuzzy →,←,→+Ⓧ,Ⓨ,Ⓧ

FISTS OF FUZZY STARTS WITH THIS SWING HIGH ...

... AND THEN PULLS BACK TO PREPARE FOR THE NEXT ONSLAUGHT. THIS IS A DIF-FICULT MOVE TO ACCOMPLISH. TRY SETTING UP A TWO-PLAYER GAME WHERE A FRIEND JUST STANDS THERE TO LET YOU GET THE SEQUENCE DOWN.

Rumble Flurry Ⓐ+Ⓑ

THE RUMBLE FLURRY FLATTENS JOHNSON HERE.

THE ONLY THING THAT CAN STOP THE FLURRY IS A QUICK COUNTER-PUNCH.

How to Beat Him

AFRO THUNDER WORKS THE BODY OF CHIN. HIT HIM ONCE AND BACK OFF. CHIN IS QUICK AND STRIKES BACK IF YOU STAY IN CLOSE.

TANK LANDS A BIG LEFT-HAND JAB. CHIN CAN TAKE A PUNCH, BUT KEEP UP THE PRESSURE. TANK CAN TAKE MORE PRESSURE THAN CHIN CAN.

BIG OVERHAND RIGHT HOOKS LIKE THIS ONE FROM BUTCHER BROWN SHATTER THAT "IRON" CHIN.

THE ROCKET'S STRENGTH IS HIS POWERFUL BODY BLOWS. THIS IS GREAT WHEN FIGHTING CHIN.

AFTER A COUPLE OF JABS TO THE BODY BY THUNDER ...

... CHIN STRIKES BACK WITH A QUICK LEFT HAND. BACK OFF TO AVOID THE ONCOMING BLOW.

Rocket Samchay

Notes

A Muay Thai champion in his home country, Rocket wants to prove to the world that his kickboxing school is the best with hands as well as feet. Although restricted with the rules of western boxing, he often punctuates his wins with eastern style fury. After studying boxing in the states and winning the championship from Angel 'Raging" Rivera, Rocket is now convinced that he is unstoppable.

The Stats

Hometown:	Bangkok, Thailand
Weight:	165 lbs.
Height:	6'2"
Reach:	78"
Age:	23

Fighting Basics

THE ROCKET IS A POWERFUL BOXER. HERE JIMMY BLOOD FEELS THE WRATH OF A VICIOUS RIGHT CROSS.

THIS LEFT JAB GETS SAMCHAY A LETTER FOR RUMBLE MODE. NORMALLY YOU CAN LAND TWO QUICK JABS BEFORE YOUR OPPONENT'S COUNTER-PUNCH ARRIVES.

SAMCHAY'S REAL STRENGTH IS HIS ABILITY TO THROW STRONG COM-BINATIONS. START OF WITH A SERIES OF BODY BLOWS LIKE THIS.

 AND FOLLOW IT UP WITH A BIG OVERHAND RIGHT.

 SAMCHAY IS A WELL-BALANCED BOXER. WITH A LITTLE BIT OF PRACTICE, YOU SHOULD BE SEEING THIS SCREEN A LOT.

 ROCKET CAN TAKE A PUNCH, BUT DON'T GET CARRIED AWAY. WHEN MOTAR ENTERS RUMBLE MODE, BACK AWAY FROM THIS LARGER BOXER.

Special Moves

Rocket Launcher →,←+Ⓧ

 THE ROCKET LAUNCHER STARTS OUT WITH SAMCHAY IN A LOW CROUCH.

 THEN SAMCHAY EXPLODES UPWARD ...

 ... TO LAND A CRUSHING UPPERCUT TO JIMMY BLOOD.

Left Elbow Smash ←,→+Ⓧ

 ROCKET SETS UP FOR A LEFT ELBOW SMASH AGAINST FAZ MOTAR.

 THE LEFT ELBOW SMASH IS A LEFT HOOK THAT HITS YOUR OPPONENT WITH AN ELBOW AS YOU SWING THROUGH.

Right Elbow Smash ←,→+Ⓨ

 THE RIGHT ELBOW SMASH IS THE SAME AS THE LEFT, JUST WITH A DIFFERENT ELBOW. HERE RIVERA GETS HIT WITH THIS SPECIAL MOVE.

Double Trouble ←,→+Ⓧ,←+Ⓨ

DOUBLE TROUBLE COMBINES THE TWO ELBOW SMASH MOVES. IT STARTS WITH THE LEFT ELBOW SMASH ...

... AND FOLLOWS IT WITH THE RIGHT ELBOW SMASH.

No Trouble →,←,→+Ⓑ

 NO TROUBLE STARTS OUT WITH ROCKET SPINNING AROUND.

 HE THEN DELIVERS A LEFT-HAND TO THE BODY ...

 ... FOLLOWED BY A QUICK RIGHT-HAND BODY SHOT.

Bangkok Express →,←,→+Ⓑ,Ⓨ

  ... ROCKET LANDS THIS UPPERCUT TO FINISH THE MOVE.

THE BANGKOK EXPRESS IS A FINISH TO NO TROUBLE. AFTER THE LAST BLOW FROM NO TROUBLE ...

Rumble Flurry Ⓐ+Ⓑ

IF YOU GET TO RUMBLE MODE AND YOU SEE AN OPENING, CALL FOR RUMBLE FLURRY.

THE DAMAGE DONE BY THE SERIES OF BLOWS IS WORTH IT.

The Fighters

53

How to Beat Him

ROCKET'S NOT VERY FAST. BLOCK HIS INITIAL SHOT.

THEN COUNTER-PUNCH. THIS WEARS SAMCHAY DOWN SO YOU CAN DEFEAT HIM.

ROCKET LIKES TO THROW A LOT OF BODY BLOWS, SO BLOCK DOWN LOW. BE CAREFUL THOUGH.

HE MAY THROW A COUPLE TO THE BODY AND FOLLOW WITH A QUICK BLOW TO THE HEAD. READ HIS BODY MOVEMENTS AND SWITCH TO THE BLOCK HIGH OR GET OUT OF THE WAY.

WHEN YOU SEE AN OPENING, TAKE IT WITH EVERYTHING YOU'VE GOT. HERE FAZ MOTAR LANDS A POWERFUL RIGHT HOOK TO EARN A LETTER AND DAZE SAMCHAY.

WORK THE BODY OF ROCKET. IT'S HIS TRUE WEAKNESS.

Bruce Blade

Notes

A skilled naval shipyard engineer and notorious ladies man, Bruce moonlights as a boxer in identity-shielding headgear. The added protection is also rumored to protect his dashing good looks, not to mention his over-inflated ego. New to professional boxing, his hit and run tactics might seem cowardly to some and have also caused critics to doubt his seriousness for the sport.

The Stats

Hometown:	San Diego, California
Weight:	243 lbs.
Height:	6'5"
Reach:	78"
Age:	25

Fighting Basics

Bruce Blade can throw one heck of a punch. He sizes up Rocket here.

Then he delivers a blow.

That one sends Samchay flying backward. The downside to Blade, however, is that he only has two quick punches. The first is the uppercut sequence shown here.

THE SECOND IS THE RIGHT-HAND JAB. ALL OF HIS OTHER MOVES ARE SLOW, SO WATCH OUT.

YOUR OPPONENT HAS TIME TO MOVE OUT OF THE WAY OR STRIKE WITH A QUICK COUNTER-PUNCH.

IN RUMBLE MODE, YOUR OPPONENT WILL BE RUNNING SCARED. BLADE IS A VERY STRONG BOXER WHOSE PUNCHES DO GREAT AMOUNTS OF DAMAGE.

Special Moves

Corkscrew Blade ←,→+Ⓧ

THE CORKSCREW BLADE STARTS BRUCE DOWN IN A CROUCH.

FROM THERE HE EXPLODES INTO A DEVAS-TATING UPPER-CUT.

Sit Down ←,←,→+Ⓨ

THE BIG UPPERCUT FROM THE RIGHT IS COMING.

IT KNOCKS SAMCHAY BACK ON HIS HEELS.

Disrespect →,→,←+Ⓨ

BRUCE PIVOTS BACK AT THE START OF THIS MOVE. BE CAREFUL; YOU ARE WIDE OPEN WHEN YOU TURN YOUR BACK.

THE RIGHT HAND THEN RAKES ACROSS THE FACE OF YOUR OPPONENT.

THE MOVE FINISHES WITH YOU WIDE OPEN. BETTER HOPE YOUR PUNCH LANDED AND YOUR OPPONENT IS HURTING.

Notes

Bruce Blade is the Champion of the Bronze Class. To get access to him, each of your gym's boxers in Championship mode will have to reach the Sliver Class. Unlock Blade in Championship mode and he'll be available in Arcade mode.

Rumble Flurry Ⓐ+Ⓑ

Your opponents will regret it when you enter RUMBLE mode.

This sequence of blows will have even the hardiest of boxers reeling.

How To Beat Him

Wait for Blade to throw a body shot. It's so slow you can dodge out of the way.

Then counter with a quick punch of your own. Use your blocks and dodges to set up almost all of Blade's punches.

Use your fighter's natural strengths against Blade. Samchay's best punch is the body blow, which he demonstrates here.

Rivera has plenty of warning to block this overhand right.

Use your special moves, like Thunder does here, to hurt this large boxer. You must hit him hard and often to knock Blade down.

When you see an opening, throw a quick jab to disrupt his rhythm.

Kemo Claw

Prima's Official Strategy Guide

Notes

Kemo is a wise old boxer who baffles opponents with his somewhat mystic fighting style. It is said he channels the spirit of the greatest warriors from his family, and that his long reach and towering height are the products of a shaman. Rarely uttering a word, his actions speak loud and clear.

The Stats

Hometown:	Gallup, New Mexico
Weight:	120 lbs.
Height:	7'1"
Reach:	99"
Age:	34

Fighting Basics

KEMO CLAW HAS A HUGE REACH. WITH THIS LANKY FIGHTER YOU CAN STRIKE YOUR OPPONENTS WITHOUT FEAR OF BEING INSIDE THEIR RANGE.

EVEN WITH HIS SLIGHT FRAME, HIS PUNCHES STILL PACK A LITTLE SOMETHING EXTRA. HERE THIS LEFT UPPERCUT SENDS RIVERA FALLING BACKWARD.

THE EXTRA REACH HELPS YOU OUT BECAUSE A LOT OF CLAW'S PUNCHES ARE A BIT SLOW. RATHER THAN STRAIGHT JABS AND HOOKS, CLAW LIKES TO SWING BACKHANDS AND CHOPS.

HOWEVER, KEMO THROWS A NORMAL LEFT JAB. WITH THE INCREASED RANGE, THIS IS A VERY EFFECTIVE PUNCH.

CLAW'S BODY BLOWS ARE EXCEPTIONALLY LONG PUNCHES. HE STARTS BY PIVOTING, LEAVING HIS BACKSIDE EXPOSED TO ATTACKS.

AFTER THE PIVOT, HE BRINGS THE PUNCH TO BUTCHER BROWN'S BODY.

Ready 2 Rumble™

Special Moves

Warcry ←,→+Ⓧ

THE WARCRY STARTS WITH CLAW BRINGING HIS HAND BACK.

HE THEN BRINGS IT FORWARD IN A BIG ARC ...

... THAT LANDS ON BORIS'S HEAD. THIS IS A VERY EFFECTIVE PUNCH.

Arrowhead Punch ←,←+Ⓧ

CLAW CROUCHES AT THE BEGINNING OF THE ARROWHEAD PUNCH.

HE FOLLOWS WITH A LURCH FORWARD WITH BOTH HANDS HELD TOGETHER ...

... AS THEY STRIKE BUTCHER BROWN IN THE CHEST.

Shaman Punch ←,←,→+Ⓨ

CLAW READIES THE SHAMAN PUNCH.

IT STARTS WITH A PIVOT BACK ...

... AND FOLLOWS WITH A BIG RIGHT HOOK.

WarPath ←,←,→+Ⓨ,Ⓑ,Ⓐ,Ⓧ

AFTER FINISHING A SHAMAN PUNCH ...

... THE MOVE EVOLVES INTO A WARPATH, WHICH HAS THIS PUNCH TO THE BODY ...

... AND THEN THIS POWERFUL LEFT HAND.

Rumble Flurry Ⓐ+Ⓑ

The Rumble Flurry catches Selene off guard and running.

But she can't outrun it and feels the power of this sequence of punches.

How to Beat Him

Kemo's long arms force you to be inside his reach to land a punch.

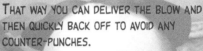

Therefore, throw punches that have your maximum reach. That way you can deliver the blow and then quickly back off to avoid any counter-punches.

To throw any kind of body punch, you must get in close.

And once you are in close, hit him with your most powerful punches. If you can stun him, you can escape before he strikes back.

It helps when you have a boxer like Butcher Brown. His most powerful punches are his right and left hooks, which you can use at a distance against Claw.

You have to plan on the counter-punch coming. Land a couple of blows and then back off. Here Boris didn't back off in time and is about to get struck with a left-hand blow.

Nat Daddy

The Stats

Hometown:	Las Vegas, Nevada
Weight:	265 lbs.
Height:	6' 9"
Reach:	100"
Age:	25

Notes

Intimidating and with an awe-inspiring presence, Nat has arrived in the boxing scene as one of the largest figures in the sport, physically and professionally. Relying on his super-long reach and frightening agility, he is regarded as a legitimate contender despite his somewhat limited arsenal of punches. Still, one can't help but think that someday, he could take the Championship belt by force.

Fighting Basics

NAT DADDY HAS GOT GREAT REACH. THIS RIGHT HOOK ...

.. SEEMS LIKE IT COULD HIT THE OTHER SIDE OF THE RING! AFRO THUNDER THOUGHT HE WAS SAFE THAT FAR BACK. HE THOUGHT WRONG.

ALL OF NAT'S PUNCHES ARE SLOW, BUT THEY'RE LIKE AN ONCOMING FREIGHT TRAIN. IF THEY HIT, SOMEONE'S DAY IS RUINED.

IT WILL TAKE A LOT TO KNOCK DOWN NAT DADDY. TAKE THE PUNCH ...

... AND COUNTER-PUNCH. ROCKET SAMCHAY FEELS THE BRUTE FORCE OF THIS UPPERCUT.

YOU WOULDN'T THINK IT, BUT NAT DADDY IS PRETTY AGILE. THIS HIGH-FLYING SPECIAL MOVE PULVERIZES SELENE.

Special Moves

Jackhammer ←,→+Ⓨ

NAT DADDY RAISES BOTH FISTS IN PREPARATION FOR A JACKHAMMER.

BOTH ARMS SWING DOWN, POISED TO STRIKE AFRO THUNDER'S CHIN.

BOTH FISTS LAND, DOUBLING THUNDER OVER.

Dropping Bombs ←,←,→+Ⓨ

DROPPING BOMBS IS A LOT LIKE A JACKHAMMER.

BOTH HANDS COME UP ...

... AND DROP LIKE BOMBS ON YOUR OPPONENT. BUTCHER BROWN FEELS THE EXPLOSION OF THIS POWERFUL MOVE.

Power Trip →,←,→+Ⓑ

POWER TRIP IS LIKE A REVERSE JACKHAMMER. YOU START IN A CROUCH ...

... AND EXPLODE UPWARD WITH BOTH FISTS.

THE RESULT IS THE SAME THOUGH. SAMCHAY IS SENT FLYING BACKWARD AFTER THE BLOW LANDS ON HIS CHIN.

Dump Truck ←,←,→+Ⓨ,Ⓑ

READY TO HAUL OUT THE TRASH? DUMP TRUCK IS A NICE COMBINATION.

IT STARTS OUT AS A SUPER JACKHAMMER WITH NAT DADDY JUMPING HIGH INTO THE AIR.

THEN BOTH FISTS CRASH DOWN JUST LIKE IN A JACKHAMMER.

BUT THEN BOTH FISTS COME BACK UP LIKE A POWER TRIP.

How to Beat Him

WORK THE BODY OF NAT DADDY. YOU HAVE TO THROW YOUR QUICK PUNCHES OR GET CAUGHT BY A COUNTER-PUNCH.

RIVERA IS QUICKER THAN NAT DADDY.

SO HIS PUNCH IS THE ONE TO LAND AND DO THE DAMAGE.

SALUA WORKS THE BODY. WHILE YOU'RE IN THERE, LAND A COUPLE OF SPECIAL MOVES OR COMBOS. IT TAKES A LOT OF BLOWS TO KNOCK NAT DADDY DOWN.

A SHORTER BOXER WITH LESS REACH (LIKE ROCKET HERE) MUST WORK INSIDE.

WATCH OUT THOUGH; NAT DADDY CAN BE SLY AND LAND A BIG RIGHT HOOK LIKE THIS ONE.

Notes

Nat Daddy is the Champion of the Silver Class. To unlock him, get all 14 boxers in Championship mode (the 13 regular boxers plus Bruce Blade) to the Gold Class. Unlock Nat in Championship mode and he'll be available in Arcade mode.

The Champ: Damien Black

The Road to the Top

You must go through the reigning Champ, Damien Black. All of your hard work comes down to one fight. Do you have what it takes? When you stare across the ring into those menacing eyes, will you blink? You must fight a nearly flawless fight to beat Damien Black. Read on to find out what you need to know.

Afro Thunder has climbed to 2nd place in the Silver Class. The only thing standing between him and the Gold Class, is Damien Black.

Damien Black is so tall (7'3'') that he doesn't even fit on the screen during the introduction!

When you are the Champ, you've earned the right to taunt and talk some trash.

You just might wind up seeing this screen a couple of times. Damien Black is one tough boxer.

Ready 2 Rumble™   Prima's Official Strategy Guide

Damien Black

Notes

Little is known about the strange abomination known as Damien Black. It is speculated that he is a being from another dimension and that he funds and promotes many boxing events, including his own. It is also rumored that the Blackheart Spear, his patented body blow, causes fighters to become ill the instant it connects. His goal is unclear, but few wish to stand in his way.

The Stats

Hometown:	Unknown
Weight:	250 lbs.
Height:	7'3"
Reach:	105"
Age:	Unknown

Fighting Basics

Damien Black is the biggest, the strongest, and has a huge reach (105"). Once you've taken each of your boxers to the rank of Champion, you can fight this awesome boxer.

Every single one of Damien's punches would flatten a novice boxer. This uppercut catches Bruce Blade and sends him flying back.

This powerful right hook is going to land squarely on Salua's round chin.

BACKED INTO A CORNER, BRUCE BLADE IS AT DAMIEN'S MERCY.

AFRO THUNDER HIT DAMIEN SQUARE WITH A BIG PUNCH. BUT LOOK AT

DAMIEN'S HEALTH BAR—HARDLY A SCRATCH! YOU CAN TAKE A TON OF PUNISHMENT WHEN FIGHTING AS BLACK. FORGET ABOUT BLOCKS.

JUST ABSORB THE BLOWS FROM YOUR OPPONENT AND KEEP ON PUNCHING.

Special Moves

Scorcher ←,→+Ⓧ

DAMIEN STARTS OUT THE SCORCHER WAY DOWN LOW.

THEN HE EXPLODES UP WITH A LEFT UPPERCUT.

THIS MOVE CAUGHT BUTCHER BROWN OFF GUARD AND SENT HIM FLYING.

Damien's Grip →,Ⓧ+Ⓨ

DAMIEN'S GRIP INVOLVES A LUNGE FORWARD, SO START A LITTLE WAYS

AWAY FROM YOUR OPPONENT. HOWEVER, THIS IS JUST A HAIR TOO FAR AWAY.

BOTH OF DAMIEN'S HANDS SWEEP IN TO BOX HIS OPPONENT'S EARS.

BUT THE MOVE WAS STARTED JUST OUT OF RANGE, AND HE MISSES.

Damien's Fury →+Ⓧ+Ⓨ,Ⓑ,Ⓐ,Ⓨ,Ⓧ

DAMIEN'S FURY STARTS WITH THE SIMPLEST OF PUNCHES ...

... A LITTLE LEFT HAND JAB.

THIS IS FOLLOWED BY A BIG OVERHAND RIGHT, THEN THE REST OF THE MOVES

THAT MAKE UP THIS DIFFICULT COMBINATION. ONCE YOU'VE UNLOCKED DAMIEN, FIGHT A TWO-PLAYER BOUT AGAINST YOURSELF AND PRACTICE THIS ONE BEFORE TRYING IT ON YOUR FRIENDS.

Pitchfork ←,→+Ⓨ

ROCKET SAMCHAY IS ABOUT TO FEEL THE WRATH OF DAMIEN'S PITCHFORK MOVE. DAMIEN WINDS UP TO BRING BOTH FISTS FORWARD ...

... JUST LIKE A PITCHFORK.

Raging Storm →,←+Ⓧ

RAGING STORM IS A BIG LEFT UPPER CUT.

DAMIEN STARTS OUT CROUCHED ...

... THEN HE LEAPS INTO THE AIR, LEADING WITH HIS LEFT HAND.

Hades ←,→+Ⓐ

DAMIEN SPINS BACK (LEAVING HIMSELF WIDE OPEN TO ATTACK) ...

... AND DELIVERS THE LEFT HAND BLOW TO TANK'S BODY.

Blackheart Spear ←,←,→+Ⓑ

THE BLACKHEART SPEAR IS A POWERFUL RIGHT HOOK. DAMIEN STARTS MOVING FORWARD, RIGHT HAND COCKED ...

... AND DELIVERS A CRUSHING BLOW TO THE HEAD OF JIMMY BLOOD.

Rumble Flurry Ⓐ+Ⓑ

DAMIEN UNLEASHES THE POWER OF RUMBLE MODE WITH HIS BATTLE CRY.

FISTS FLY, DEALING OUT PUNISHMENT ...

... BLOW BY BLOW.

How to Beat Him

WHEN YOU FIGHT AGAINST DAMIEN FOR THE CHAMPIONSHIP, HE HAS TONS OF SPECIAL MOVES THAT YOU DON'T HAVE WHEN YOU FIGHT AS HIM.

ABSORB THE HIT AND THEN DISH OUT A COUNTER-PUNCH TO TEACH HIM A LESSON.

BEFORE YOU FIGHT FOR THE CHAMPIONSHIP, MAKE SURE YOU HIT THE WEIGHTS TO INCREASE YOUR STRENGTH. AS YOU GET STRONGER, YOU CAN ABSORB MORE PUNCHES.

BIG MOVES, LIKE THIS LEFT UPPER-CUT FROM AFRO THUNDER, ARE WHAT YOU NEED TO KNOCK OUT THE CHAMP.

AN ADDED BONUS TO THROWING THE BIG MOVES IS THAT YOU COLLECT LETTERS FAST. THAT GETS YOU TO RUMBLE MODE WHERE YOU CAN PILE ON THE PUNISHMENT.

WHEN FIGHTING FOR THE TOP SPOT IN CHAMPIONSHIP MODE, YOU NEED A BOXER WITH STATS LIKE THIS. PRIZE FIGHTS GET YOU THE CASH SO YOU CAN TRAIN HARD ENOUGH TO ACHIEVE THESE STATISTICAL LEVELS.

You've got to get through Bruce Blade and Nat Daddy (the Bronze and Silver Class champs) to get to Damien.

The fight against Bruce is just the prep work for fighting Damien. Keep training and you'll be ready.

The Last Fight

After 29 Title Fights, countless hours in training, and numerous Prize Fights, it all comes down to one fight. Damien Black holds the Gold Class belt. You were good enough to take the Bronze and Silver belts away from him. Can you beat him one last time?

To beat Damien Black for the Gold Class Championship, you must have a very special boxer. You must train long hours in the gym (strength better be near 100 percent) to even think about getting into the ring this time. But then, if you've made it this far, you probably have that good of a fighter. Pick one good punch (like Afro Thunder's sweeping left uppercut) and throw it repeatedly. Your strength, stamina, dexterity, and experience will keep you in the fight while he punishes you with counter-punches.

Persistence will win the fight. The punch you pick should be one that earns you letters. It should do tons of damage, then you can pile it on in RUMBLE mode.

The former Champ is down for good. Now you get to call yourself Champ, the best of the best.

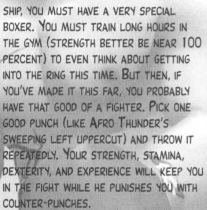

A perfect 40-0 record.

In the Gym
Championship Mode

The second gameplay option in *Ready 2 Rumble* is Championship mode. The object of this mode is to train and guide each of your fighters from Bronze Class to Championship level. You start out the game with three fighters in your gym: Boris Knokimov, Butcher Brown, and Afro Thunder. Each boxer has four stats: strength, stamina, dexterity, and experience.

To get your boxers to the Championship level, you must fight Title Fights to move ahead in the ranking. In order to do that, you must increase your four stats from their initial zero value. You do that by training your boxer and fighting in Exhibition and Prize Fights. This section of the guide explains how to get from your initial stable of three fighters at Bronze level to all of your fighters as Champs.

ONCE YOU GET TO 1ST PLACE OF THE BRONZE CLASS, YOU MOVE UP TO THE SILVER BRACKET. YOU START OUT IN SILVER, FIGHTING FOR 10TH PLACE.

IN A PRIZE FIGHT, MONEY IS ON THE LINE. WIN AND YOU GET THE $2,000 PURSE PLUS WHATEVER YOU BET ON THE FIGHT.

YOU CAN BUILD YOUR BOXER'S STATS BY PURCHASING TRAINING PROGRAMS. HERE IS A PICTURE OF THE SPEED BAG MINIGAME WHERE YOU CAN IMPROVE YOUR BOXER'S DEXTERITY AND STAMINA.

THIS IS THE MAIN MENU SCREEN IN CHAMPIONSHIP MODE. YOU CAN CHOOSE TO TRAIN YOUR BOXER; FIGHT TITLE, PRIZE AND EXHIBITION FIGHTS; OR TRADE A BOXER TO ANOTHER GYM.

THE OBJECT OF CHAMPIONSHIP MODE IS TO GET ALL OF YOUR BOXERS FROM BRONZE CLASS TO CHAMPIONSHIP LEVEL. YOU MUST FIGHT A LOT OF FIGHTS TO ACCOMPLISH THIS.

ONCE YOUR FIGHTER IS RANKED SECOND, THE NEXT FIGHT IS AGAINST BRUCE BLADE FOR THE TITLE IN SILVER CLASS.

TIP

To run a successful gym, you need money. So your first step should be to take one of your boxers (whoever you feel most comfortable with) and fight five quick Prize Fights. Each time, bet the maximum wager. Then switch to another fighter and do five quick Prize Fights with him, again betting the maximum wager. Now train that first fighter. I recommend concentrating on strength training, so head for the weight lifting program. Strength helps your fighter absorb your opponent's punches during the fight and causes your punches to strike that much harder. Once you've gotten your strength up, head on over to the speed bag and build up your stamina and dexterity.

Now you have a boxer who can cruise through the Bronze Class. Take that fighter all the way to the top of Bronze, and start the process over with your other fighters. This method should get all of your boxers to the top and allow you to have a nearly undefeated record.

Train Your Boxer

Your four stats (strength, stamina, dexterity, and experience) all start out at zero. To improve the first three, you must train your boxer. *Ready 2 Rumble* has six minigames that give your stats a boost. But training costs money, which you can earn with Prize Fights.

THIS IS AN INITIAL BOXER STAT SCREEN. EVERYTHING IS AT ZERO RIGHT NOW.

TRAIN YOUR BOXER TO BECOME A BETTER FIGHTER AND INCREASE YOUR CHANCES OF WINNING.

THE WEIGHT LIFTING PROGRAM BOOSTS YOUR STRENGTH, MAKING YOU A BETTER BOXER. STRONGER BOXERS CAN DEAL MORE POWERFUL BLOWS AND ABSORB THE PUNISHMENT HANDED OUT BY OPPONENTS.

A BETTER STAT SCREEN

The amount your stats increase is variable. Each time the minigame is played, the game predetermines how much the stats can increase. If you select Auto Training, your stats increase at 100 percent of that amount. If you select Manual Training, the increase depends on how well you can play the minigame. Do well and you can earn up to 150 percent of the increase. Do poorly and you only earn 50 percent.

At the end of a Manual Training session, the game tells you what percentage you received and gives you a ranking. The exact break point on the ranking changes each time you play a minigame, so 115 percent might give you a Bruiser ranking one time but a Bouncer the next. Here's a listing of the ranks you can earn for a training session:

- Keep Practicing
- Weakling
- Wannabe
- Trainee
- Novice

- Bouncer
- Bruiser
- Contender
- Champ
- Rumble Master

FINISH UP YOUR TRAINING TO BE RANKED IN THIS SCREEN. YOU MUST EXECUTE THE TRAINING MISSION PERFECTLY TO BE A RUMBLE MASTER.

Rumble Aerobics Training

With Rumble Aerobics Training, you can increase your boxer's stamina and dexterity. Stamina increases by about 0.2 points on average, and dexterity picks up about 0.5 points. The little bouncing ball moves from left to right. Press the corresponding key when the ball bounces on top of it. If you time it right, the button will darken. Miss and it stays bright. The mini game ends when you fail to complete three patterns, so stay sharp. Your ranking and training percentage goes up each time you successfully complete a pattern.

Ready 2 Rumble™ Prima's Official Strategy Guide

Copy patterns like this one. Press the correct key when the little bouncing ball lands on a letter.

Keep it up. This is a near successful pattern completed. Your stats increase with each pattern done correctly.

Sway Bag Training

Sway Bag Training works on your boxer's stamina and dexterity. Stamina gains a paltry 0.3 points on average, and dexterity picks up around a full point. The way Sway Bag Training works is by giving you a pattern of moves to memorize. You start out the training with a left jab to get the bag moving. Then on subsequent patterns, you start swaying left, right, and back. Pay close attention to the pattern. If you mess up and get hit by the bag, the training is over. Obviously the more patterns you make, the more training points you receive.

The first punch is a left jab (⊗) to get the bag moving.

After the first punch, you're given a larger sequence to memorize.

Follow the pattern— a sway to the right to avoid the bag.

The training program is over when you miss the pattern and get hit by the sway bag. Like all other training modes, you get ranked to determine how big of a stat increase you get.

Speed Bag Training

Speed Bag Training increases your stamina and dexterity. Stamina picks up about 1.2 points while dexterity picks up 0.5 points. The object of the game is to get the speed bag to swing and hit the ceiling. Start out with a jab. When the bag starts to swing forward, hit the bag again. After a couple of hits, the bag begins to hit the ceiling. Make sure you time your hit when the bag is just starting to head away from you.

In addition to a jab, you can also throw a right hook. This gets the bag moving faster, but it also takes more energy away. When the red power bar decreases all the way to the left, the training mode is over.

Use jabs (X or Y) to get the bag moving.

The speed bag swings away from you, then swings back in your direction. When it starts to fall away from you again, hit it with another jab. Repeat the process to get the bag really moving.

You must do really well on this minigame to get a good score. Here, the bag hit the ceiling 39 times, which is only good for a Weakling ranking.

Heavy Bag Training

Heavy Bag Training works your boxer's strength, stamina, and dexterity. Strength is the big winner with a heavy bag session, gaining around 4 points. Stamina gets about a 0.6 increase, and dexterity picks up about 0.5 points on average. Your trainer calls out a punch, and you have to throw that punch as quickly as possible. If the red time bar runs out or you press the wrong button, you miss. Three misses and the training session is over.

Work the heavy bag to improve your strength, stamina, and dexterity. Your trainer will call out a punch and you have to press the corresponding key.

Weight Lifting Training

Weight Lifting Training adds to your fighter's strength and stamina. Strength goes up 7.2 points on average, and stamina goes up about 0.5 points. This is the most affordable way to increase your strength. The object of the game is to lift the weights as efficiently as possible. Press and hold (A) to start lifting the weights. Try to release (A) when the white bar reaches the top green line. The weights and the white bar start to come down. Press (A) again to stop the weights close to the bottom green line and start the next rep.

Press and hold (A) to start the weights (and the white bar) moving up.

Release (A) so the white bar stops as close as possible to the top green bar.

Then press and hold (A) again as the white bar falls toward the bottom green line. Your efficiency is graded on how well you can accomplish this feat.

Your efficiency is judged by how close you can get to starting and stopping at the two green lines. Lifting efficiently means you lose less power and can do more reps. Weight Lifting Training is over once your power bar decreases to zero.

Do it well, kid, and you could be a contender.

Vitamin Training Program

The Vitamin Training Program has no minigame. Buy it for $10,000 and you increase your stamina and dexterity. Stamina increases about 1.2 points, and dexterity goes up 1.5 points. While Vitamin Training seems to do a lot with one dose, it's not all it's cracked up to be. You can purchase six Speed Bag Training workouts for $9,500 total and get about 7.2 points of Stamina and 3 points of dexterity. Now that's more bang for your buck.

The Vitamin Training Program gives your fighter better stamina and dexterity. With increased stamina, your punch's power bar increases faster, so you can throw more punches.

But your training dollars are better spent over at the speed bag.

Rumble Mass Nutrition Regime

Rumble Mass Nutrition Regime is another training program with no minigame. This program increases your strength and experience. You pick up about 14 points of strength and 7.5 points of experience for the $25,000 that this program costs. This program is the only one that adds to your fighter's experience total, so it's very attractive in the early stages of the game. Your money would be better spent elsewhere if it weren't for the added experience, which normally can only be picked up in fights. I recommend doing this once or twice in the beginning, but after you get fighting experience behind you, concentrate on weight lifting to up your strength.

Rumble Mass Nutrition Regime increases your strength and experience. Your punches now have just a little more bang.

Normally the only way to gain experience is through fights. Rumble Mass adds to your experience in the beginning part of the game—a good way to jump start your fighter's career.

After a couple doses of Rumble Mass, go back to weight lifting. You get more for your money there.

Title Fight

Title Fights are where you attempt to move your boxer up in rank. The boxer starts out as an unranked Bronze Class fighter, and the first fight is for 10th place. With each win, you move up one spot. Once you win the fight for 1st place of Bronze Class, you become an unranked Silver Class. Fight all the way to the top of Silver, and your fighter becomes an unranked Gold Class fighter.

• The entry fee for a Title Fight is $2,000 for Bronze Class, $3,000 for Silver Class, and $5,000 for Gold Class. You must fight Prize Fights to gain your entry fee.

• Before fighting your first Title Fight, fight a number of Prize Fights to gain money for your gym. With the money, you can train your boxer to boost stats.

• If you lose a fight, don't panic; these things happen. Just make sure you have enough total fights left to fight for 1st place. If you don't, go back to a previous save because the boxer gets reset when the number of fights left hits zero.

• As you move up in rank and class, the location of your fight changes. Also, hardly anyone attends the fight for 10th place of Bronze Class, but the house is packed by the time you are fighting for 1st place.

Caution

You have a limit of 20 total fights (Title, Prize, and Exhibition) for each boxer to move from one class to another. If you run out of fights and haven't reached the next class, your fighter drops back down to an unranked Bronze, and all the stats get reset to zero.

TAKE A LOOK AT THE CROWD IN THE BACKGROUND. THERE AREN'T MANY PEOPLE BACK THERE FOR YOUR LOW-RANKED BRONZE FIGHTER'S FIRST COUPLE OF FIGHTS. OH WELL, ONLY THE PRIVILEGED FEW CAN SAY THEY KNEW YOU WHEN.

BUT AS YOUR FIGHTER ASCENDS THE LADDER, THE CROWDS BUILD.

AND WHEN YOU REACH THE FIGHT FOR 1ST PLACE, THE ARENA IS BIGGER, AND IT'S PACKED.

OUCH, THAT'S GOTTA HURT! BUT WITH IMPROVED STATS YOU CAN ABSORB MORE OF THESE BLOWS DURING A FIGHT. GET INTO THAT GYM AND DO SOME TRAINING BEFORE YOU HEAD OUT FOR A TITLE FIGHT.

BRUCE BLADE IS THE BRONZE CHAMP. BEAT HIM AND YOU'RE ON TO SILVER, WHERE NAT DADDY REIGNS. GET PAST HIM AND YOU'LL FACE DAMIEN BLACK!

WINNING

YOU MAY FACE A SETBACK OR TWO ON YOUR WAY TO THE TOP. DON'T WORRY THOUGH, THAT'S WHY THE DESIGNERS GAVE YOU 20 FIGHTS TO MOVE FROM UNRANKED ALL THE WAY TO 1ST.

Prize Fight

Your gym needs money to train your boxers and pay the entry fees to Title Fights. The way you gain more money is to fight Prize Fights against the computer or Exhibition Fights against boxers from your friend's gym.

With a Prize Fight, $2,000 is the purse. You may also increase the amount you can win by placing a side bet up to the amount of money your gym has, or $20,000, whichever is lower. To get your gym ahead, fight five Prize Fights for two of your boxers and bet all the money you have (or the $20,000 maximum when you're at that point). This pool of money allows you to train your boxers and cruise through the Bronze Class on your way to the Championship level.

WHEN YOU FIGHT A PRIZE FIGHT, $2,000 IS UP FOR GRABS— THAT AND ANY MONEY YOU PUT DOWN AS A SIDE BET. HERE THE WAGER WAS $4,000, MAKING THE FIGHT WORTH $6,000

YOUR GYM'S BANK ACCOUNT.

PLACE YOUR BET UP TO $20,000. BET THE MAXIMUM TO BUILD UP

Start this process of doing five quick Prize Fights once you get one boxer to the Silver Class. Each time one of your fighters reaches Silver Class, a new boxer is unlocked and added to your gym. This new boxer is an unranked Bronze Class fighter. Once all 13 boxers are available, Bruce Blade is added. Once all 14 boxers reach Silver Class, Kemo Claw becomes available. Get everyone to Gold Class, and Nat Daddy is added. To get Damien Black, everyone will have to be a Champion. Once you get a boxer unlocked in Championship mode, the boxer will be available in Arcade mode as well.

PRIZE FIGHTS TAKE PLACE IN A SMALL LITTLE GYM LIKE THIS ONE.

YOU WON THE FIGHT.

NOW USE THAT MONEY YOU WON FOR TRAINING.

Exhibition Fight

An Exhibition Fight is where you get to pit a boxer from your gym against a fighter from a friend's gym. When you fight an Exhibition Fight, both fighters agree on a wager and fight for that purse. Someone is going to lose money on this fight, so don't go crazy with the betting. While you can be reasonably sure of your ability to beat the computer, your friend could have been practicing and might surprise you.

MENU WITH EXHIBITION SELECTED

SELECTING THE WAGER

NOTE

When the bosses are unlocked in a gym, they are available in Arcade Mode. Reload that gym when you turn on the system.

KNOCKED DOWN ...

... AND KNOCKED OUT.

Caution

Whenever you're knocked down, you automatically gain some health back (except for the last knockdown). If you rapidly press any of the buttons, you get *more* health back. The only time you or your opponent won't get up after a knockdown is when the maximum knockdown value is reached. This can be set under "options" for Arcade mode, but is always the same value (three) in Championship mode.

Trade Boxer

You can trade a boxer from one gym to another. This can be very useful. You can fight a large number of Prize Fights to train a particular boxer on one saved game, then trade that boxer to the gym where you are storing trained boxers. You could also trade a boxer to a friend to help start out a new gym.

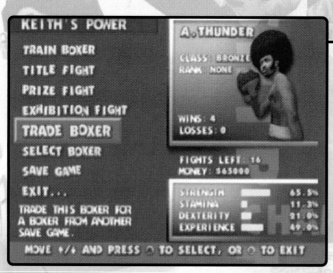

YOU CAN TRADE A BOXER FROM ONE SAVE GAME TO ANOTHER VIA THIS TRADE BOXER MENU.

USE ONE GYM TO FIGHT PRIZE FIGHTS AND BUILD UP YOUR BOXERS. THEN TRADE THEM TO A GYM WHERE YOU'RE STORING YOUR TRAINED FIGHTERS. YOU CAN ALSO TRADE A BOXER TO A FRIEND TO HELP THEM OUT.

Other Platforms

PlayStation

The PlayStation version of the game plays exactly the same as the Sega Dreamcast version, only with fewer polygons for the models. You can translate the codes from the "Roll Call of Fighters" section, and they will work just as well. But the folks at Midway wanted to give PlayStation owners a unique feature. That feature is the inclusion of Gino Stiletto™.

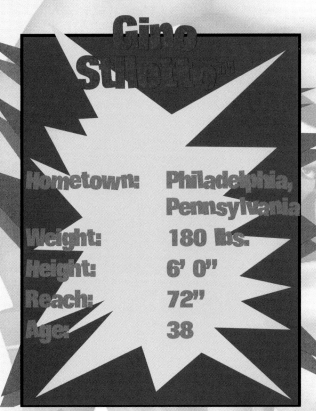

Gino Stiletto™

Hometown: Philadelphia, Pennsylvania

Weight: 180 lbs.

Height: 6' 0"

Reach: 72"

Age: 38

Gino is a proven warrior whose accomplishments are some of the most noted highlights in the sport today. He has won and lost the championship many times, often coming out of retirement to do so. Now a respected trainer, his star pupil, J.R. Flurry™, carries on his testament, but the success Gino's protégé garners has rekindled a fire thought long extinguished. Donning his trademark Stars and Stripes, Gino reenters the pugilist world for perhaps the last time.

THE ROAD TO THE CHAMPIONSHIP BELT IS STILL THE SAME. YOU MUST GET THROUGH THE THREE CHAMPS TO WIN IT ALL. DON'T WORRY THOUGH. ALL OF THE MOVES ARE THE SAME IN THE PLAYSTATION VERSION AS IN THE SEGA DREAMCAST.

TRAIN YOUR BOXER TO GET A SUPERIOR FIGHTER. ALL THE STRATEGIES THAT WORK ON THE SEGA DREAMCAST WORK ON THE PLAYSTATION.

NOTE

The final move list for Gino Stiletto was not yet nailed down when this book went to print. When the PSX version hits the store shelves, check out *www.primagames.com* to find the move list and some screen shots for this new fighter.

Nintendo 64

The N64 version of the game plays exactly the same as the Sega Dreamcast and PlayStation versions. As with the PlayStation, you can translate all of the moves from "Roll Call of Fighters" to work on the N64. The fighter list changes a little bit more though. Jimmy Blood isn't on this version, but J.R. Flurry takes his place.

J.R. Flurry™

Hometown: Los Angeles, California
Weight: 160 lbs.
Height: 5'11"
Reach: 75"
Age: 21

A star athlete in high school and college, not to mention a sought-after personal trainer throughout Hollywood, J.R. traded in his certification when he met boxing great Gino Stiletto. Being under Gino's wing has awakened a natural champion and crowd favorite who has taken the boxing world by storm. Armed with a stiff jab and a lightning fast one-two combination, J.R. is easily amongst the elite in the sport.

THE N64 VERSION IS IDENTICAL IN FEATURES TO THE SEGA DREAMCAST. ALL THE MOVES AND STRATEGIES ARE THE SAME.

HERE JET CHIN AND SALUA SQUARE OFF IN A MATCH ON THE N64.

NOTE

The final move list for J.R. Flurry was not yet nailed down when this book went to print. When the N64 version starts arriving in stores, go to *www.primagames.com* to find the move list for this fighter, as well as a couple of screenshots.

Codes

What would a game be without codes? Here's your guide for unlocking the hidden features inside *Ready 2 Rumble*. These codes must be activated before selecting your boxer.

Alternate Costumes

From the Character Select screen, press Ⓧ+Ⓨ to fight wearing the boxers' alternate costumes.

HERE'S BUTCHER BROWN IN THE DEFAULT BLACK TRUNKS AND WHITE TRIM.

HERE HE IS IN BLUE TRUNKS WITH GREEN TRIM. PRESS Ⓧ+Ⓨ FROM THE CHARACTER SELECT SCREEN TO FIGHT IN THIS OUTFIT.

Choose a Cornerman

During each bout, your fighter hears advice from a cornerman. Like one voice over another? Then press Ⓧ + any direction to pick out one. Execute this code at the Character Select screen.

The Leprechaun

Need a laugh during the fight? Then press Ⓧ+Ⓛ+Ⓡ from the Character Select screen to hear this unusual cornerman.

Choose an Arena

YOU CAN PICK WHERE YOU FIGHT. ONE OF THE PLACES IS THIS LARGE ARENA.

In two-Player mode, press either Ⓛ (two-tier arena), Ⓡ (Championship arena), or Ⓛ+Ⓡ (gym) to select the arena where you wish to fight.

Fighter Access

Need a little help in Championship mode? Here are some codes to give you a hand.

Gym Name	Access
Rumble Power	Bronze Class
Rumble Bumble	Silver Class
Mosma!	Gold Class
Pod 5!	Champ Class

ENTER THE GYM NAME FROM THIS SCREEN ...

... TO GAIN A STABLE OF HIGHER-CLASS BOXERS.